"...And then she had it all"

Arannya
and the
Four leaf clover

Bhavana poly

BLUEROSE PUBLISHERS
India | U.K.

Copyright © Bhavana Poly 2025

All rights reserved by the author. No part of this publication may be reproduced, stored in a retrieval system or transmitted in any form or by any means, electronic, mechanical, photocopying, recording or otherwise, without the prior permission of the author. Although every precaution has been taken to verify the accuracy of the information contained herein, the publisher assumes no responsibility for any errors or omissions. No liability is assumed for damages that may result from the use of information contained within.

BlueRose Publishers takes no responsibility for any damages, losses, or liabilities that may arise from the use or misuse of the information, products, or services provided in this publication.

For permissions requests or inquiries regarding this publication, please contact:

BLUEROSE PUBLISHERS
www.BlueRoseONE.com
info@bluerosepublishers.com
+91 8882 898 898
+4407342408967

ISBN: 978-93-6452-163-5

Cover design: Yash Singhal
Typesetting: Namrata Saini

First Edition: February 2025

Dedication

Forever in debt to all the sacrifices my parents Mrs. Sarita and Mr. Arvind Kapse made to support me and my brother, Mr. Pankaj Kapse, to become who we are—two thriving opinionated good samaritans. Without your blessing, nothing of this would have been possible.

> In loving memory of my Mama
> Late. Mr. K.B.Bhagatkar.

To my younger self, "As promised I have not let the writer inside me die!"

And, to those beautiful eyes reading this, Thank you for giving my words a chance.

Love and Light!

Contents

Present Day 1

Story of the four leaf clover 3

Luck 8

Faith 20

Hope 47

The Metamorphosis 84

Love 93

Finding the four leaf clover 282

Present Day

Thick, dark, and red, the floor is covered in blood; one could hear banging on the door and people screaming outside the bathroom. After a few attempts, the door is broken open; everyone is aghast to see Arannya lying unconscious on the floor, blood oozing out of her hand profusely.

A night before the big day.

It was the Devil's hour when the phone buzzed ferociously: grrrr...grrrr...grrrr.

Only a few minutes ago she dived into deep sleep. Her mind had already entered into the subconscious stage, but one part of the brain was still receptive to what was happening in the surroundings. 'Open the eyes,' the mind was signalling her, but she was in another episode of sleep paralysis.

After struggling for a few minutes, she opened her eyes and reached out to get her phone; it was tucked under her sister's bum.

"Sleep, Aaru, there's a lot to do tomorrow." Saying that, her sister turned towards the other side, and she grabbed her phone. It was a number that was not saved in her contacts, but she could remember it even in her next life, if there is one.

With some trepidation, she unlocked her phone; there was a voicemail that said, *"We met with an accident."*

It was a bolt from the blue for her! She struggled to breathe heavily, so shocked that she couldn't move an inch. She could feel her brain fading, as if she was turning into a rock.

What she heard in the voice note devastated her.

They say be careful of what you wish for; was it because she wished for something like this? Can she have it all? Or had she just lost everything?

It is her wedding tomorrow!

Story of the four leaf clover

Arannya, a name made up of her parents' names conjugated, Arun and Ananya. Some people called her Aarya because they couldn't make efforts to say her full name; some called her Aaruna; and the people closest to her called her Aaru. But she liked to be addressed as Aarna, for in her childhood she struggled to pronounce her name completely and ended up babbling when asked what her name was as "Aar...nnna.".

Resembling any girl of her age, she too was full of curiosity since childhood. Being an only child and having working parents with less time to spend with her, all her childhood memories were with her 'Dadu,' her grandpa.

Ever since she started to walk and talk, she always had her Dadu to look after her. She grew up listening to the stories of revolutions, magicians, old folklore, and great scientists. He was her everything, her superman, in a nutshell.

And then one day, the vices of old age knocked on Dadu, and he was found to be terminally ill.

Arannya was only eleven to understand the pain of loss. She used to ask him to go on evening walks, but he started to become weak and pale as days of his heavenly abode approached.

"Aaru," that's what Dadu used to call her.

One serene afternoon, he asked her to read him a book; she obliged and read from his favourite author, Munshi Premchand ji's Idgah.

After every story Dadu used to recite to her, he would close it with a moral takeaway.

"You see, Aaru, true love is not just the extravagant gestures one does for you once in a blue moon, but having someone in your life who looks after your needs and puts your needs first; it's then you realise the true meaning of love and life."

"But Dadu, what if I never found such a person?" She asked sadly.

Dadu caressed her and pulled her cheek and kissed his fingers. And said

"Then, darling, you become that person."

This was something that had a deeper impression on her than someone of her age could fathom. Like her soul's purpose.

"Dadu, you have read so many stories and books and have travelled and met so many people. Why don't you tell me your own story? Today you have to tell me a story of your own." Aaru ordered. It was like a royal decree for him, and he cannot decline it. But what should he tell her? He couldn't come up with any story. He rolled his eyes around his room in an attempt to find something, then a bunch of wildly grown clovers caught his attention.

And he began to somehow weave a story around it and narrated, "This is '*The Story of a Four Leaf Clover.*'"

This was the time when there was no currency and humans were yet to discover the barter system. People used to find happiness with the sun rising every morning and the changing phases of the moon. Receiving rains on time, plucking flowers and fruits to eat. Back in those days, the only prized possession was being alive and surviving. But in every community, small or largely established, there used to be a person who people used to look upon for guidance and support. In every Kabila, there used to be one such person who was considered the luckiest, based upon the fact that he'd found the Four Leaf Clover.

Reason being, it was a very rare phenomenon to find one with four lobes. You may find the ones with three lobes everywhere, but a four-leaf clover was something to be cherished for. Since Earth was still fresh before human evolution destroyed it, the four-leaf clover during that time was very large in size, just like a leaf in the cornfield. And when someone finds it, luck starts to be on their side. Nothing could go wrong with the person possessing the four-leaf clover. He'd never be sick. Live a long life full of abundance, happiness, and love.

Each lobe was a representation of Luck, Faith, Hope, and Love. Even today, people still believe that it brings good luck. But nature has its way to teach the simpleton human that not everyone can have all four; hence, you can find the three-leaf clover commonly but not the one with a four leaf. Which puts each one of us into either one of the four categories; one could have the other three and still be either hopeless, faithless, luckless, or loveless.

Only a few chosen ones would fall into the fifth category, which is being hopeful, faithful, lucky, and loved.

Given his age, he was mostly blabbering and was half asleep already, but Arannya was listening to him keenly.

"Dadu, have you found the four-leaf clover?" she asked curiously.

Dadu was fast asleep by the time she asked this. But she couldn't stop pondering about the four-leaf clover. She thought, Will she ever be able to find one? The next day in the morning, she woke up and saw a bunch of people gathered in his room. She rushed in and saw her dad sitting next to Dadu. Her dad was sobbing.

Dadu's eyes were stuck on the ceiling, and his mouth was open; he was counting his last breaths. Her dad called her near him and asked her to pour some water in his mouth. She could see his tongue was rolled back, but his pupil turned towards her.

"Dadu, tell me, did you find the four-leaf clover?" A curious child, unbothered about the delicacy of the situation, asked this of her dying grandpa.

In response, he tried hard to nod and blink his eyes in affirmation and touched her face before he finally said goodbye to this world.

Ever since, Arannya has tried hard to search for the four-leaf clover in every nook and cranny of Dadu's room, every page of the book, every pocket of his pants and shirts, and the trunk he kept safe, which was a gift to him by Dadi, who unfortunately she never saw. But sadly, she couldn't find the four-leaf clover.

As she grew older, her memories with her grandpa started to fade away from her mind, and only a few made their way to her core memory. One of which was the moral of the Idgah story he told, and another was the story of the four-leaf clover.

Until the day she reached her grandpa's age, she didn't realise what it truly meant.

Luck

*L*uck is something everyone is born with. Good or bad makes the whole difference. But there are certain things where it does not discriminate. Like death, it doesn't matter to which side of the luck you fall; when the time comes, every breathing entity has to sleep on its lap. Apart from death, another thing where this phenomenon applies is a person's first love.

First love never succeeds! This is not just a saying but an axiom; someone has acquired all the worldly knowledge when this was coined.

In the balance of life, death and first love are that state of the equilibrium where it does injustice to both the lucky and the unlucky ones.

Even the luckiest people have faced defeat at the dawn of love.

She was in 6th grade when her classmates made an advancement in their conversation from different storybooks, comics of 'Chacha Chaudhary,' Marks, episodes of Aladdin, and Disney's Recess, which was her personal favourite cartoon; That's so Raven, Hannah Montana, dolls, Sunday's family outing, new additions in the wardrobe, glitter pens, pens with 5 different colours, etc., to "Boys"!!!!

Oh, are they even a topic to discuss? They are the opposite gender, always on the other side of the fence. What are they supposed to do in a girl's world? She would wonder.

What is it like to befriend a boy? She never had this curiosity, nor did she ever think of anything above and beyond studies and mull over what she was going to eat at her next supper.

Having grown up in an Asian household, "love" was a taboo topic; she could hardly remember where the word "love" was even used in any conversation until her intermediate years, when she was confronted by her mother after she laid her hands on a greeting card Arannya received. "Do you love him?" her mother asked.

Arannya was filled with shame as if she got caught doing something despicable!

It was in one of the drawing classes when she became part of a conversation where girls of her class were chit-chatting about how Ruby and Vishal are "girlfriend-boyfriend."

How can Vishal give Ruby a set of glitter pens that had twenty-four colours? Can someone really do that even when it's not another person's birthday? She was amazed.

That day she went home musing upon why these girls were talking about forbidden things like love and boys and not sticking to usual gossip about Saas-Bahu drama, which was prominent then, and all girls used to watch it sneaking alongside their moms. The resurrection of the male protagonist for the third time seemed logical and was always a hot topic!

In the night she talked to herself and decided that she was going to stay away from such topics and focus on her academics, but little did she know that Cupid in her life was already waiting for her with his strings drawn. This was her first experience with the feeling called love and the Cupid's first arrow; out of who knows how many?!

The next day at lunch break, the same group of gossip girls gathered and started to talk about the Lovebirds, Ruby and Vishal; this time, to her surprise, even Ruby was a part of it!

"You know he calls me Rooh, and I have nicknamed him Wish," said Ruby. "Oh my God!" they all exclaimed in unison. "These guys are living life in a true sense," said Priya. Arannya remained quiet in disbelief. How can Ruby shamelessly accept that she is dating Vishal? Doesn't she care about her reputation?

Thud!!! A ball made up of a boy's tie hit Arannya's head. "Ouch," she groaned, scratched her head, and ruined her ponytail in the process. A boy came running towards the girls; everyone was staring at him. Arannya picked up the ball and returned it to the boy; she was fuming, "Sorry, Arannya." He took the ball and ran back to his flock of boys who were playing dodgeball with that thing.

"Is he not Sajan? From section C," Navya asked, who was from section B, Arannya's classmate.

"Yes, of course he is; I know him well, as he sticks around with my Wish most of the time, more like a third wheel to us." Ruby sounded pompous. "Sorry, Arannya!!! How does he know her name?" She continued to chatter.

"Yeah, I'm sure he doesn't know my name or Radhika's name," said Navya.

"Hmmm, Arannya, what's cooking?" They all pulled her leg, and she was baffled how to react to this. This was a new type of emotion for her of embarrassment and of pride at the same time.

Walking back to the class, she had the same question knocking in her head: "How did he know my name?" He was a new admission in the school this year, and there wasn't ever a time when these two shared anything, be it a PT session. Anyway, who cares, she thought, and blew off the question just like blowing the remains of the pencil waste from the sharpener and tightened her loose ponytail.

On the same day after school, when these girls were walking back to their homes, Navya asked Ruby, "So what are you doing this Saturday?" Ruby said she is going to watch Basic Instinct at Vishal's house while his parents will be away for some work. Since Saturday was a half day at school, Ruby planned to lie to her parents that she would be attending extra classes and sneak into Wish's place.

This time Arannya did not feel low about Ruby; in fact, she was surprised by her boldness. She was intrigued by the way Ruby was risking her reputation all for the person she "loves"! Isn't that strange and amazing? Ruby has now become a symbol of style and an idol for Arannya and the rest of the girls in the group. They reached the midway point where the girls had to split their ways. "By the way, Arannya, Saajan was asking about you," Ruby told her. "About me? Why?" She tried hard to hide her excitement, but smartass Ruby got her. "Oh ho oh, look at the blush, hahaha," she laughed and went on her way.

It was too late by the time she realised that something had changed in her; she was naive to not understand that this little mindless teasing was going to affect her significantly. That night she couldn't sleep peacefully, or let us say the previous night was the last time she slept peacefully.

Adolescence was about to spring.

After a few days, when Arannya was monitoring the class and waiting for the math teacher to come and take over, she heard someone at the door say, "May I come in, teacher?" and everybody started laughing; yes, it was him, Sajan! He deliberately called her 'teacher' just to look funny. When Arannya saw him, she became nervous; her hands were sweating, but she was feeling different in a good way! Like that feeling when all eyes are on you and it just makes you feel wonderful? This was the first time she felt special.

Since this day her world changed; there were different feelings and emotions running inside her; she could feel more alive. "How does he know my name?" "Did he really ask about me to Vishal?" "Did he come to the class to have fun or just to see me?"

Her mind was infiltrated with Sajan's thoughts. And her peers added fuel to the fire; when she entered the classroom, a few boys would sing songs with his name in them: *"Saajanji ghar aaye, saajanji ghar aaye, Arannya kyon sharmaaye saajanji ghar aaye?"* and the whole class would split into laughter.

In a few other instances, during one of the lunch breaks, Sajan walked to her and asked if she'd like to exchange her lunch box with him since he's got bitter gourd and she agreed to it happily gulping the sour curry just for him. He was performing a dare given to him by his friends otherwise he'd have to treat them with chinese food after school. But Arannya's intuition was getting stronger by his gimmicks. In one of the classes, he visited their section and passed a textbook to her and asked if she could give it to Vishal, who was sitting in closer proximity to Sajan, and the way he smiled looking at her added fuel to the speculations.

All of this started to affect Arannya in ways more than she had thought. Most of her time went dwelling on thoughts about how it would be to become someone's girlfriend. After her name was tagged with Sajan, she had gained popularity in the school as well. She secretly enjoyed the attention.

Her friends and the gossip girls left no stone unturned to make her believe that Sajan has a crush on her and that he is going to propose to her soon.

Naive Arannya started to weave her own world inside her mind that she has found her "love". Days passed like these, with many other instances where Sajan would drop hints that he was actually interested in her. The first time they spoke to each other was during the final examination's last test of Art when she forgot to carry her sketch pen packet. She panicked and couldn't understand how to deal with this situation. She was standing in the corridor while everyone else was already inside the class when Sajan walked past.

"What's the matter?" he asked,

"I forgot to carry my sketch pen set; I don't know how. What will I do? The exam is about to start." She looked worried, almost on the verge of crying; this was their first mano-a-mano. But they converse in such a way as if they've known each other quite well.

"Okay, don't worry; you take mine," he said.

"What? No? What will you do?" She was puzzled.

"Don't worry about that; I will manage; take it!" He insisted.

"Are you sure?"

He did not reply; this time, He held her hand and forcefully handed over the set to her and went inside his class.

After the exam got over, she rushed out to give the sketch pen back and say thank you to Sajan, but she couldn't find him. Ruby came by and asked who she was looking for. "I am looking for Sajan; I wanted to return this to him," she said. "No problem, I will give it to Vishal; he will give it back to him," said Ruby. "No! I will give it back to him. I want to thank him." Arannya rushed out of the school building to find him on the ground.

She went near the school gate too, but she couldn't find him. Ruby asked her to leave for home along with her, but she refused.

She stayed back in school an hour after it got dispersed. PT Master asked her who she was waiting for, and she said her mom would come to pick her up. But when everyone left the school and she could see only the peon uncle, she gave in and left for home. This was the time when 'social media' was a very distant thing. Owning a handphone was a luxury limited only to grownups, and for the rest, there were landlines.

Since that was the last exam, it meant summer holidays were ahead, and schoolmates would see each other only after two months.

During the summer break, when all her classmates were enjoying their vacation, Arannya was waiting eagerly for the holidays to get over. The way Sajan came to her rescue and saved her made her strongly believe that this is something special. As there was no mode of direct communication, all she could do was wait until she saw him again.

There were times when she made lame excuses and went to the market with her driver and saw every other boy around in the hope of bumping into him. But that's the thing about life: it has its own course. She never saw him.

Twas the night before the next term in school, and Arannya could not rest for a second thinking about going to school the next day and finally being able to convey her gratitude to Sajan. She had kept the sketch pen set very carefully, as if it was some prized possession. She was praying to God to let both of them be in the same section this time. She was full of faith that God would accept her request, as she has always been an obedient god fearing child.

The next morning she was up around 4:30 am; she bathed, got ready, put on the new hairband, saw herself longer than usual in the mirror, sneakingly applied Mum's perfume, took the nicely kept sketch pen set, and set off to school on her bicycle. She learnt to ride a bicycle during her summer break.

"Bye, Mummy," she said and rode off.

With all the gung-ho, she parked her "Miss Universe" bicycle in the stand. After the class assembly was over, the students were meant to go and sit in the same section as they were in class 6th, but in the 7th-grade classroom.

One of the teachers came and started to call the names of the pupils and assigned them their respective sections. Arannya got the same section, sec. B, and others were splitting and going to their respective classes. Her eyes were roving here and there to find him, but she couldn't. By this time she knew that he was not in her class. It made her sad.

In the short break, she enquired with her ex-classmates, who were now in different sections, if Saajan was in their section. And they gave the response she did not want to hear, "No."

If he wasn't in their class as well, then where might he have gone? Did he flunk in 6th grade? He was an average student, though! Her mind was filled with all sorts of thoughts.

She had a premonition.

After the school dispersed, she and Ruby were waiting for Vishal. Ruby was now her good pal and a classmate too. Vishal came, and Ruby went with him sideways to talk in private. After their conversation, which lasted for a few minutes, Vishal came and said, "We have to find a new 'bakara' for you, Arannya; your Sajan got transferred from the school."

Arannya's throat became dry; she could not comprehend what she heard. This news pinched her heart, leaving her sad and numb. "Hey! Just chill; let's go; otherwise we will be late for our tuition classes," said Ruby.

When Arannya came back home, she locked herself in her room and cried. After all, that's all she could do; very easily, Vishal and Ruby rubbed off the topic as if it was nothing. But for her, it was her 'love,' for what she knew at that age. She had already planned in her mind so much about them being together, just like 'Rooh & Wish,' that it gave her a feeling of failing an exam she was sure she'd top.

She was heartbroken even without having a heartfelt odyssey!

That night she did not have her food. She was hating everything in and around her and was getting irritated by even the smallest inconvenience. She learnt that "love" doesn't come to someone so ordinary. As love is a feeling so special, it will come to those who are special, unlike her. Her first experience of love was so saddening that she was terrified of loving and losing again.

They say nobody can steal your fate, but at this point in time, Arannya felt, What if she has this power!? She could steal Ruby's fate; a wave of jealousy ran through her and squeezed her stomach.

She went into self-doubt; she pondered how Vishal made efforts to win Ruby's heart and did everything possible to be around her and meet her even on Sundays. If Sajan had wanted to, he would have at least informed her that he was leaving, but maybe he never really cared about her; all his stunts were for pure fun. She thought maybe she wasn't as beautiful as Ruby; maybe she wasn't attractive enough to interest him.

This was the time her Dadu told her the story of a four-leaf clover and that of Idgah.

"Then darling, you become that person."

"Love is not for the ordinary," a voice echoed in her head.

Faith

Faith is the thing that breeds on a person's spiritual persuasion. Largely driven by a person's luck, faith can form both negative and positive notions. We tend to believe that since our luck is such, all that the future has to render will be in a similar fashion. This builds the foundation of a person's belief system.

A human has no control over the outcomes of the future events of his life. All his futile efforts of not being this and never doing that seem useless in the eyes of fate.

No matter how hard you try, if you have been boarded in a certain train, you will have to travel through everything it has to go through, including all the beautiful rivers, bridges, hills, waterfalls, fields and as well as harrowing long, almost infinite tunnels along the way. You cannot be deported at your wish, but can you at your will?

The first experience of a teenage love stint makes a person believe how his life would be in matters of the heart.

Faith is a dangerously marvellous thing. When directed properly, it can move the mountains, and when one is deprived of it, he cannot even lift a cotton ball.

Love and faith are codependent; if there is faith, there ought to be love, and if there is love, there has to be faith. Without each other, they are just like a wick without fire.

But what will happen when one's faith towards the immortal power above battles for the mortal being on earth?

Ever heard that the latter has won?

It's now been three years since her very first experience with the thing called love. After the poignant incident in her life, she had shut all the possible doors or even peepholes to the thing called love. It was very difficult for her to forget about it, but with time she finally had to let go of the bitterness it caused. She was introduced to puberty. She got her period last year, and through her biology class got to know that there are two openings in a girl's vagina, one from where they pee and the other from where they bleed, and get the babies out and how! She, by this time, has learnt that babies are not born from performing 'pooja/havan' during marriages but from intercourse.

She hated to know the process of making babies. And was scornful towards her parents for what they did in order for her to take birth. It took her a while to make peace with the fact that this is all just natural and not a thing to be disgusted with, but society still chose to keep these topics under a veil of morality, while it's all about fornication under that veil most of the time.

It was the 10th board, and she was well focused on scoring a distinction in her exams. She got section B again, and by this time the only thing that happened best to her was she found a best friend, Shiney. Shiney got transferred to her school in 10th grade.

One day while coming back from school, Arannya's bicycles chain came off, and Shiney offered to help. This incident quickly blossomed into a beautiful friendship.

When they learnt that they stayed close by, they planned to meet on a Sunday at Arannya's place.

They used to play songs on the computer, play trump cards, make drawings, and do many DIYs while watching Art Attack on the Disney Channel. They became close and confined their fears, dreams, and ambitions to each other. Arannya knew it was a pure friendship when she told Shiney everything about Sajan and her buried feelings towards him, and she did not judge her but cursed Sajan so badly that they both ended up laughing and cursing him more.

This was the beginning of a friendship that lasted forever.

One evening after coming out of the tuition classes, Arannya and Shiney were having this conversation about the newly made couples in their school. By this time, Ruby and Vishal were not seeing each other any more.

'Aarna, don't you feel it's time for you to find someone and put your feminine wiles to the test?" Asked Shiney.

"What? What's gotten into you? You know I'm doomed in this area. Let's just focus on trigonometry more because if this time we pass on the boundary, my mom will kick me out of the boundary!" Arannya replied.

"Oh, come on, Aarna, take the plunge; not everyone is an arsehole like your first love."

Arannya did not like Shiney calling him that. She still secretly hoped that someday Sajan would show up.

"Shiney I know you are dating Nayan and having a ball, but trust me, I am least interested in indulging in anything but studies right now! And I think you should do the same."

Shiney stopped trying to persuade her further on this topic.

After a few weeks in school, during recess time, a group of girls was having their lunch.

"Hi Shiney, what did you get in your tiffin?" Asked Ruby.

"Brinjal curry and chapati," Shiney answered.

"Let's eat together," Ruby said. And Arannya also joined them.

Arannya could notice that the girls were talking more to Shiney; she felt left out. After their lunch, the same gossip gang was talking about something, and this time in a very low voice. Even though Arannya was close by, she could barely hear anything, and they were talking in code words too. There was a girl named Kinjal. She was known for her bitchiness. Even she joined the gossip, and when Arannya asked, "What are you guys talking about?" Kinjal said arrogantly, "Girl! First, get a boyfriend to get involved in such discussions. This is no kid zone; you better watch Pogo!" and everyone in the group laughed at her.

Why did they laugh at her? They were a group of girls infamous for their affairs; even the teachers did not like them. What made them feel so proud about it, and why did they belittle her?

The times have changed. Arannya was so busy shutting her feelings down that she forgot she was growing, and along with her, her desires were growing too, which she thought would never resurface. But in this moment she was feeling so envious about these infamous girls that she just wanted to punch them hard and run away. She looked at Shiney, and Shiney's eyes were saying out loud, "I told you! It is time!"

On their way back home after school, Arannya was angry and confronted Shiney because she also played a part in laughing at her when Kinjal made that sinister remark on her.

"So now you'll laugh at me, huh!?" She was clearly disappointed.

"I didn't mean to Aaru, but it was so spontaneous that I couldn't stop myself and gave in to the situation. I am so sorry to hurt you." Shiney apologised.

Arannya did not say anything and left towards her home.

This was one of those nights when she questioned herself. Sajan did not reciprocate the way she wanted; she is still single; no boy has ever signalled her or proposed to her! Even Shiney is dating someone. This broke her confidence; she felt she was not good enough to attract boys. She must be really very common, or Vanilla, as the girls would tag single girls. Being rich is not the only thing that'll make you attractive at this innocent age. It terrified her. She did not want to be tagged as Vanilla, as she knew she was more than that. The thought of being left out disturbed her. She was at the peak of self-doubt and baloney.

Arannya was not able to focus on her studies; she started to look at boys and see if anyone was looking back at her, but there was no one. Not even the ones who were not smart enough. She became insecure. She thought about speaking about this to Shiney many times, but she was too shy to initiate this conversation, as she herself warned Shiney not to talk about such things with her.

But Shiney got her. She noticed Arannya was not her usual self and seemed to be distant most of the time. She decided to confront her after their tuition classes. They used to go and eat snacks at their regular place, a small shop for daily needs, and a cafe.

"Aaru, is something disturbing you?" Shiney asked.

"No! Why do you ask?" she replied.

"Just like that." Shiney said and passed her a mango juice tetra pack.

'Aarna, tomorrow is a Saturday, and we are planning to bunk the classes and go for a ride on our scooter; will you join us?" Shiney asked. Shiney was still in touch with her ex-schoolmates and used to meet them quite often, but this was the first time she asked her to join in.

This was Arannya's chance to mingle with new people, especially boys. Without a second thought, she agreed. "It's going to be fun!" Shiney was euphoric.

The next day, as planned, both Shiney and Arannya were waiting for Shiney's friends to come near the cafe. This shop was their 'joint' or 'adda.' Both the girls had an amazing bond with the shop owner, Tinku Bhaiya, and they even used to take things on credit as well.

"Here they are!" Shiney rejoiced as she saw her boyfriend speeding towards her on his bike. There were two more guys; one was Ganesh, and the other was Kartik.

Ganesh put his sturdy-looking sports bike on a stand and came near Arannya.

"It is time," Arannya told herself.

"Hi, I am Ganesh. Nice to meet you, umm." He tried to recall her name but couldn't.

"Arannya," said another guy. Arannya tilted her head to see the boy who came on a scooter, unlike Ganesh and Nayan.

"Okay, okay! Cut the introduction part and let us go before any of our classmates see us," said Shiney. Saying so, she hopped on the Nayans bike and left Arannya confused.

"Hey! Where are you going? You come with me!" Arannya said to Shiney.

"We are not taking our scooter, Aaru; you are a pillion to Ganesh."

"Wait, what? No, I won't; you come with me, please." Arannya insisted, but Shiney did not budge an inch; she had orchestrated this situation so that she could set her up with Ganesh.

"Hurry up and sit behind Ganesh," Shiney said and rode off with Nayan.

Arannya was in an awkward situation; she was left with no choice as Shiney took her scooter keys with her. Shilly-shallying, she went near Ganesh and asked him how she was supposed to sit on his tall bike, as she had never sat on a sports bike before.

Kartik, who was still there watching all this, got down from his scooter and said in a very neutral tone, "See, you need to put your left leg on the footrest, lift your body, and sit; that's it!"

"I have never sat on such a bike before; what if I fall down?" She was afraid.

After exchanging some glances between Ganesh and Kartik, she asked if she could ride Kartik's scooter and if he could come with Ganesh.

Since they had already wasted ten minutes, Ganesh agreed with the arrangement, but he wasn't happy as he thought Arannya would sit on his bike.

Kartik gave the keys to her, and she rode off. Ganesh made sure that he did not lose sight of her and was riding behind her.

After a half-hour drive, they all reached 'Adam-Eve' Dhaba. Shiney and her friends have been frequent visitors here.

It was a garden-style dhaba on the highway, and there were small open huts that had a cot inside to sit and eat in. Shiney and Nayan have already called the restaurant and booked one hut for all of them.

Arannya tried hard to gel, but being an introvert, she was finding it difficult to fit in. And this was the first time that she had bunked her classes and came this far away from the city. She was constantly looking at her watch so that she wouldn't lose track of time, as they have to go back home on time.

Kartik, who also seemed a little disconnected from the gang, was observing Arannya without her noticing it.

"Guys, I am out of cigarettes; anyone else want some?" Kartik asked.

"Bro, get one mild for me," said Ganesh.

"Come, Aarna, let's go." He took Arannya by surprise.

Arannya was amazed, and her heart started to beat abnormally. He didn't call her 'Arannya' but 'Aarna'; only her close friend would call her that. She looked at Shiney, and she said, "Yeah, go along; anyway, you are being a spoilsport." Arannya felt bad and wished she could escape the awkwardness; accompanying Kartik was the escape she needed.

"There is a pan shop just a few meters away from the dhaba. Hope you won't mind walking a little." Kartik said.

This was the time Arannya saw him properly. Kartik was wearing a black and ash gingham shirt and black jeans, with sleeves half folded. As he was walking ahead of her, she could notice that he had a well-chiselled body, he was fairer than her, he was wearing branded shoes, and he had a typical right-side-tilted walk. Plus, he was smelling like chocolate.

He suddenly turned back, and she stopped.

"Walk faster; what are you doing checking me out!?" Kartik's voice was very masculine for his age. Adam's apple did him right.

"Sorry?" Arannya was perplexed.

"Just kidding, dude, are you always this serious?"

She chose not to reply. After walking along the sidewalks for two minutes, they reached the betel leaf shop. Kartik bought cigarettes with some mint-flavoured chewing gum, and they started to walk back to Dhaba.

Arannya was getting more awkward as she thought Kartik would speak to her, but he did not speak much.

They reached the Dhabas entrance. "While going back, I will be riding my scooter; if you want, you can come with me." Kartik said this to Arannya and walked inside.

Arannya felt something different when he said that, like a feeling of kama muta. She got confused about how to feel about that; she was happy and anxious, whatever it was; she felt good. And she blushed as she could feel the tingling sensation in her stomach.

It was sunset, the day surrendered to the evening; everyone had a great time. Arannya finally opened up and made friends with Shiney's boyfriend Nayan, along with Ganesh, and of course Kartik.

Ganesh was hopeful he could persuade her; he had asked Kartik if he could drive his own scooter and ask Arannya to sit with him. Kartik agreed to this. Ganesh started his bike and signalled Kartik to tell Aarna to sit with him.

"Guys, I have some work in between, so I will go on my own scooter." Kartik said.

"Ok, no problem, I'll drop Aarna," said Ganesh.

"I will go on a scooter only; I am afraid of sitting on bikes; I will sit behind Kartik." Aarna affirmed.

Ganesh seemed sceptical about this; he suspected Kartik must have planned it this way, but that was so unlikely of him, as he has always maintained distance from girls. Arannya hopped behind Kartik, held the seat bar behind, and they drove off.

During the ride, they did not say anything until it started to rain out of nowhere. As they were outside the city, it wasn't wise for them to stop by, so all of them continued to ride. Shiney and Nayan passed by them; Shiney was holding Nayan tight.

Arannya was completely drenched and started to shiver. Kartik applied the brakes abruptly.

"You are shivering! like this, you will get sick; I don't have a jacket as well!" He was concerned.

"It's OK; I will manage; just keep on riding." Arannya was struggling to talk.

Kartik lifted the stand, but he didn't start the scooter.

"What happened?" asked Arannya.

Kartik took her hand, wrapped it around his waist, and started the scooter.

Arannya couldn't say anything; he was holding her hands with his left hand so that she wouldn't take them away. She strangely felt warm and wonderful. Even in the cold, windy, rainy weather, she felt warm. And maybe Kartik might have felt the comfort too.

They rode like this for another 20 minutes until they reached the cafe from where they started their journey. Her eyes were closed as the raindrops were hitting hard, and she was not able to wipe them since her hands were "cuffed." She did not realise she was holding him the rest of the ride.

"We reached," whispered Kartik to her in a very low and soft voice, unusual for his voice quality. She opened her eyes and saw it stopped raining. A bit embarrassed, she took her hands off him and got down off his scooter.

Everyone arrived; their clothes were moist. It was time to say goodbye.

"OK, guys, you girls go back to your home since the weather is bad and it can start to pour again. We will also head back." Said Ganesh.

"Bye everyone, see you guys soon," said Shiney and hugged Nayan.

Kartik and Arannya were stealing glances while the others were chit-chatting.

"Bye, Kartik." She waved at him.

"Dasvidaniya." he waved back.

"What is Dasvidaniya?" Arannya asked Shiney when the boys left; she told her it's a Russian word for goodbye, which literally means 'Until we meet next time.'

"Until we meet next time!" Arannya came home and went straight to the washroom, took a shower, changed her clothes, wore a nice, cosy Looney Tunes gown, and slid under the blanket. "Until we meet next time!" When will it be the next time? She was adrenalised.

She could feel something inside her body was changing; she couldn't forget the feeling when Kartik took her hand and wrapped it around himself. Every time she was thinking about that ride, oxytocin was being released in large amounts in her brain.

This was the era of black-and-white phones, when every emotion had to be put in words with no emojis apart from the ones made out of semicolons and round brackets. Her phone chimed; it was a text from an unknown number.

"Hope you reached safely."

It was from Kartik, the first boy on her contact list.

She was on the seventh sky and jumped like a kangaroo, like she won something in a raffle draw. Her housemaid snooped, but Arannya traded carefully and made her believe it's one of those lame jokes her friends send over text and nothing else.

It was Friday again, and she was expecting Shiney to meet her friends, but this time Shiney went to visit her grandparents, and Arannya lost hope of meeting Kartik. She did not want to come out as needy; hence, she refrained from texting Kartik, and that's exactly what he thought and did not text her.

She decided to wait until the next day, and if he doesn't text her, she should just put off the growing feelings towards him.

On Saturday, after her tuition classes, she went to Tinku Bhaiya's shop, where she used to park her scooter. She was hungry and wanted to eat some cream rolls.

"Tinku Bhaiya?" She called.

No answer. "Tinku Bhaiya, are you there?" Still no answer. How can he leave the shop open and go? she wondered.

"Yes, Aarna?" Said a familiar voice, but definitely not Tinku Bhaiyas.

She turned around, and her face instantly lit up. It was like her prayers were answered, and she was having a big smile on her face.

It was, Kartik!

They saw each other; their eyes were shining, and butterflies were dancing in their stomachs. For them, they thought it was love, but it was their puberty on duty gushing them up with dopamine!

"You? What are you doing here?" she asked.

"Just came to buy some cream rolls!" Kartik winked.

"OK, where is Tinku Bhaiya?" she asked.

"He went on a bio break; ah, there he is." Kartik pointed to Tinku Bhaiya, who was coming towards the shop adjusting his pants.

They sat and had coffee along with cream rolls. Kartik showed his new phone with a camera that his parents gifted him as he topped in the unit test again.

It was 4:30 in the evening, and the weather was ambient. Kartik got Arannya some chocolates; he knew Temptations Rum n Raisin was her favourite. She was beaming. While leaving, Kartik locked his right pinky finger with her left-hand pinky finger and took a photo. He even kept that as his wallpaper.

This marked the beginning of her first love tale.

Arannya was the happiest girl; she finally felt that she was the main character of her story, not some ordinary person. Kartik made her believe that she was a special girl. The gossip girls gang started to see her off highly, as she was dating one of the most handsome guys in their circle. He was a school topper and leader of his school as well.

Kartik, on the other hand, was so mesmerised with Arannya that somehow his day's schedule got modified, and seeing her was at the top of his to-do list. Since his school would disperse half an hour before hers, he made sure that he would ride to her school to see her.

Every day he would get something or the other for her; at times it would be a map stencil, which she said she needed to buy, a rose to help her smooth sail from her pre-menstruations, a logbook, chocolates, mathematics notes, and of course a set of glitter pens. Arannya now knew why exactly someone could give the whole set to someone.

The days were passing by, and their boards were commencing. It was high time for them to shift their focus from their sweet little love story towards physics, chemistry, and mathematics, which she dreaded. Even during these days, Kartik would make sure he met her at least once after her tuition classes. But, in this, she unconsciously sidelined Shiney, as the time she used to spend with her was now Kartik's. But Arannya was so blind to this that she did not realise it until Kartik was gone from her life!

It was her birthday, and her friends had made plans for her without her knowledge. It was a Saturday, and they planned to go to 'Adam-Eve,' the place where Kartik and Arannya first met. After their tuition, Shiney and Nayan came near the cafe. Shiney bunked her tuition for making the arrangements for her birthday. Arannya was angry as she did not accompany her to the classes. After she came out of the class, she saw both of them, and Shiney came to wish her happy birthday and hugged her. After a while, Ganesh also came with his girlfriend Kritika; she was in 9th grade. But Arannya's eyes were searching for Kartik. He wasn't there.

"We know who you are searching for!" Said Ganesh by looking at her disappointed face.

"Where is he?" she asked.

"He is attending his extra classes; he said he will come, but it will be late for him, so we will be going to Adam-Eves, and he'll join us shortly," said Ganesh.

"No! Shiney, can you call him and check with him? He is supposed to be here, where these extra classes came in between." Arannya told Shiney.

"Aaru, he will come; trust me; for now, let's go." Shiney assured her.

"I am not going to drive today! I want him to come and take me there," Arannya threw tantrums.

"I will ride your scooter, baby; you sit behind me," Shiney said in a voice convincing enough for Arannya to be her pillion.

After a silent half-hour drive, they reached their destination. Arannya was taken by surprise to see the whole hut decorated in red heart-shaped balloons and a birthday banner with her name, a birthday cake that had a happy birthday topper that said, "My life". Arannya was emotional seeing all this; all her anger at Kartik just disappeared in a second.

"OK, where is he?" she asked with tears of happiness in her eyes. She could see Ganesh and Nayan murmuring about something.

"What happened, guys? Where is Kartik?" Arannya was concerned now.

"We couldn't reach his number; he must be on his way." Said Ganesh.

Arannya tried calling him; she could hear his caller tune that sang, 'Tere hi liye, tujhse hu juda, jannatein kahan bin hue fanaa,' but there was no response from the other end.

She tried three times but got no response; she could feel something was not right. Everyone was waiting for Kartik to come. Arannya was walking to and fro; her eyes were at the entrance.

After a while her phone chimed; there was a message from Kartik, *'Aaru I met with an accident.'*

She got furious; she was convinced that he was pulling off a prank again since he was late. Arannya was waiting for him to show up and then take him to task. After 10 more minutes, Ganesh enquired, "Aarna, did you speak to him?"

"No! But I got a text from him, and I'm so mad that I am going to kill him once he is here!"

"What did he say?" Asked Shiney.

She showed her his text, and Shiney shouted at her, "Are you for real? What if this is true?"

Her heart sank. She started calling him continuously but got no response.

All of them left from there to see where Kartik was, and on their way back, Arannya got a call from him. "Kartik, what the hell, where are you? I hate you; where are you? We are coming there." But what she heard from the other side dried her blood at once.

"He is in the hospital; I'm his sister."

Arannya usually had a pessimistic approach towards life. All she could think of was the worst. While her heart was struggling hard to believe that everything was fine and it was just an accident.

They reached the hospital; the place was crowded, and people were gathered around Kartik's family. Arannya reached out to his sister, "Didi, where is Kartik? How is he?"

"Are you Aarna?" His mother asked, and Arannya nodded in response.

"It was all because of this girl; it was because of this girl that my son is in this condition. Go away, you shameless girl." His mother shouted and burst out in tears.

Arannya couldn't understand a thing; she was numb. Kartik's sister took her away from there.

"Didi, what did I do? How is Kartik? Can I see him?" Arannya asked as she cried terribly.

"Aarna Kartik got hit by a truck and lost consciousness after a concussion. Doctors are treating him, but... I am so afraid." Saying this, she hugged her, and they both cried. Arannya lost her sense of judgement on what was happening around her. She never met Kartik's sister before, but she felt as if she was a part of her own family.

"Kartikkkkkk" A loud voice came from inside the hospital; his sister ran inside, but Arannya's feet were glued to the ground.

"I am going to leave this world before you; I deserve some peace in my life, which in this life with you doesn't seem possible." Kartik used to tease her.

She closed her eyes; she could feel the nerves in her brain shrinking. "Aaru, we should be having a Christian wedding. I want to see you in that white gown, walking down the aisle while I see you and cry."

"Aaru, we would have twins; okay, I don't want you to go through the labour pain twice."

"Aarna, I want to do great in my life and give you all the happiness in the world."

"Aaru, you are mine; remember that?"

Kartik's words were echoing in her head. Shiney came and took her near their scooter.

"What's wrong, Shiney? Tell me what happened to Kartik."

"Aaru, we have to leave right now," said Shiney, as she started the scooter.

Arannya, refused to leave, and rushed inside the hospital; she saw Kartik on a stretcher, his head covered in blood, he was unconscious.

"*He's gone, he's gone.*" she heard someone from the crowd yell that.

Arannya fell on the ground and lost consciousness.

Kartik was gone.

"Life is nothing but the dance of death," Karthik used to say.

For Arannya, it was a loss unimaginable. By losing him, she lost herself too. Her parents knew he was her friend, but he was her world, her present, and her future. It was difficult for her to move over the fact that he is no more. How could she ever be able to move on from him, for they have painted their entire future together? How is she supposed to move on when moving forward in life means walking with Kartik? It was as if she was paralysed.

Boards were a few months away, and Arannya stopped going to her classes. Everyone got a month off from school for their preparations; she would be home all day, locked in her room, telling her parents that she was studying, but all she did was cry each and every day.

Like Kartik's mother, she too blamed herself for Kartik's death. After all, this happened when he was coming to meet her.

Even after such a huge accident, the only person he texted was her. She was dying of guilt.

She has lost interest in everything. Her belief in being cursed rooted deeply inside her. She never celebrated her birthday ever again.

One thing that helped her hold on to herself was friendship. Shiney was no less than a lifesaver, motivator, entertainer, teacher, and, at last, a friend who was always beside her. Arannya realised that she ignored Shiney while Kartik was there, and she apologised too. Shiney was one such person in her life who was just too good to be true. She loved her, cared for her, protected her, and, above all, was nonjudgmental towards her. Apart from Shiney, Nayan, Ganesh, and Kritika turned out to be the biggest support for her during this difficult time.

To a certain extent, it's only friendship that can heal the wounds of love.

She somehow managed to secure decent marks. She would have achieved more if the situation had been different, but this was the best she could do.

The next two years passed at the speed of light. And her 12th board results were out too.

Shiney surprisingly scored the highest marks in their group; she secured 92%, and Arannya secured 89%. She scored the lowest in mathematics and managed to pass on the boundary.

Her parents, both being top-tier lawyers, wanted her to pursue law like them and join their firm. But she hated the profession, seeing her parents being busy and taking not-so-ethical approaches to win the cases. She decided to pursue engineering and fulfil Kartik's dream.

It was his dream to become a mechanical engineer and join IES. Foolish for a girl like her to choose mechanical, as she could only understand addition and subtraction. And Mechanical was all about the demonic Sine, Cos, and Theta, with bigger demons combined with theories of machines, structures, and fluid mechanics waiting for her.

But she went ahead with her decision and turned her parents' expectations down. For the first two years, her father did not even talk to her.

Shiney's father was strict on her and wanted her to become a chartered accountant, but she wanted to pursue the arts. He told her he'd only pay for her studies if she was going to pursue her career as a CA. If she wanted to pursue art, then she would be married off. She had no choice but to agree to what her father said. Arannya, on the other hand, rebelled against her parents and, being the only child, won her argument.

Even the best lawyers lose when it comes to their children.

Arannya chose to study at the same college as her grandpa, which was situated in another city.

The night before her train, Shiney visited her; both were heavy-hearted.

"Done with your packing?"

"Yeah, last-minute checkups," Arannya avoided eye contact.

"Took everything you need?"

"Yes, I guess." Again, Arannya made no eye contact.

"You forgot to pack me, idiot," Shiney said with a teary eye; her voice became heavy.

Arannya was avoiding the situation as she was not prepared to handle goodbyes.

"Hmm," is all she replied, avoiding eye contact again.

"Don't forget me," Shiney said and held her hand. Arannya couldn't control it anymore, and they hugged each other and cried their hearts out.

"Take care of yourself, Aaru. I won't be around, but I will be just a call away."

"You too, be careful and safe, Shine. Please call me every day."

"Of course I will do that."

"Okay, you go home now. I will reach out and text you." Arannya hugged her.

"Bye, Aaru."

"Goodbye, Shine."

They both wanted to say, "I love you," to each other, but they didn't. Often saying I love you to people and friends not so close is easier than saying so to our really close ones. It's one of the most difficult or awkward tasks to do.

Arannya and Shiney made promises of seeing each other at least once every two months, doing video calls every weekend, and talking every day on the phone. They were unaware that when life takes over, we often tend to lose touch with our true selves, let alone be with our closest friends.

Arannya had a handful of experiences in life by this time; she was mature enough to be on her own and explore what life has to offer her. Before starting her new life, she reminded herself that she can excel in her academics, but she should always keep her distance from love.

She had faith in her fate and acquiesced that *"love is not for the ordinary."*

Hope

The world sustains on hope, is a known perception. A person who has never won a game keeps on trying his luck year after year with the hope that one day he'll win it. And one day he does too, but was it his hope that made him a victor, or his faith in the superpower, or the skills that he honed over the time? When a person's luck is doomed at certain things and eventually his faith fades away, the only thing that keeps him going is hope. A hope that some day things will turn in his favour. And when they finally do, he is hoodwinked into believing that he's lucky and rebuilds his worn-out faith.

Even a person counting his last breaths hopes that he tricks death and lives; the people sitting on a plane pray to the almighty and hope to survive, even after hearing "May Day." Or how one refuses to believe that they've been cheated on by their love of life, hoping it all is a lie. How tragicomic!

You see, hope is a funny thing as it is powerful.

But to what extent can one rely on this fragile swindler?

Four years later, Arannya now holds a mechanical engineering degree, but her hidden love for creativity made her switch into designing. After taking up a few trendy courses, she got her first job in a firm that does architecture and building design for top-notch clientele. Though her parents kept her loaded with money, the feeling of spending her own hard-earned money gave her the kick.

She's grown into a beautiful girl with womanhood blessing her curves; fairly tall, radiant skin, bright, shiny dewy eyes, and a natural fall of hair made her a desirable catch. But the most attractive part was that, even after being so charismatic, she was single. Her mysterious aura either chickened men out or made them believe that she's taken.

This was the era when dating sites were taking over social media apps, and you could find people forging their identity and looking out for hookups. But Arannya was unbothered by these, as she was convinced that love is not in her cards.

Arannya recently moved to a flat, which she shared with the other two girls, Shiba, who was an air hostess, and Fatima, who was a college faculty member. Both were polar opposites and at loggerheads over trivial matters. Shiba used to drink, smoke, and party all night, while Fatima used to sleep by 10. Arannya played an arbitrator. After a couple of months, they managed to be comfortable in each other's company. Arannya and Shiba shared the master bedroom. Arannya's mundane life was going to change radically after Shiba got her signed up for the dating app 'Flechazo.'

It was dinner time, and since nobody wished to cook, they ordered pizza.

"Aarna, why don't you have a boyfriend?" asked Shiba.

"I don't need one," she replied and sipped the cold drink.

Fatima was at her usual best, an unbothered onlooker.

"What do you mean you don't need a boy! How are you managing your sex life?"

"I don't feel the need for it," answered Arannya.

"Don't tell me you're a virgin!" Shiba asked, squeezing her eyes

"Is that a crime?" Arannya questioned back.

"Oh, in seven hell it is! I'm literally living with nuns." Shiba rolled her eyes and passed an annoying expression. All three of them burst into laughter.

It was 2 a.m. in the night when the street dogs decided to take revenge on people and started to bark tumultuously. It broke Arannya's sleep; she got irritated. She saw Shiba was awake and was smoking on the balcony; she drank some water and joined her.

"So the dogs were successful in their mission?" Shiba giggled.

"Hmm," Arannya replied unenthusiastically.

"Want a drag?"

"Just one."

"Aaru, have you never fallen in love?"

"Of course I did, once bitten and twice shy!"

"Are you serious? When was that?"

"More than six years now."

"What the actual fuck! Girl, you have no idea what you are missing in your life!" Said Shiba as she rubbed the cigarette butt in the ashtray.

"Babe, go out, get laid! Just live your life for God's sake! He has blessed you with such beauty; don't disappoint the Good Lord. Put your feminine wiles to the test." Shiba said.

She's heard that before.

"I don't think I'm made for this hook-up culture, Shiba. I'm a demisexual. I will just get married to whoever my parents will choose for me," Arannya told.

"Dude. You gotta be kidding me; you want to save yourself for your husband? You have no idea how many chicks he would have slept with!? Aarna, Marriage is an inevitable catastrophe, and once you are married, you can just think of being with someone else. Imagine sleeping with the same man for the rest of your life! Doesn't that scare you?" Shiba said and put out the cigarette.

Arannya had a hard time sleeping that night; she had almost forgotten the feeling of being "touched." Strangely, she did not miss Kartik but the feeling of being with him. Days like these make her question herself: Was she living her life to the fullest? She has kept the doors to her heart locked; was she really missing out on things in her life?

She has no hopes in matters of the heart; she tried her luck twice and failed; she has dropped the subject from her thoughts.

But she was yet to meet the true love of her life, which was going to change her entire perception towards love and towards herself at large.

The next morning, Shiba helped her make a fake profile on the dating site 'Flechazo.' As Arannya was concerned about her identity getting exposed to unwanted people, Shiba put some random Indonesian girls' pictures, and the interest started to flood in her inbox. Shiba said they'll surf the profiles in the evening after work and fix a date for Arannya. Arannya wasn't really sure about all this; since it was a new experience for her, she played along.

Arannya had a comparatively less busy day in the office, so to kill time she opened the application. She was fascinated to know there are so many people on the app. She accepted one profile request named 'Zavian,' and she was 'Alizeh.' As soon as she accepted the request, her phone chimed.

"Hi Alizeh, how's life?"

"Hi Zavian, life's good; how about yours?"

"May I ask what you are looking for in this app?" asked Zavian.

"I'm looking for someone to spend my boring weekends with; what about you?"

"To be honest, I'm here for some fun!" said Zavian with a wink emoji.

She knew what he meant and went offline.

She was on lunch break when this conversation took place. After her work, she had to attend a high tea with her colleagues as they successfully got approvals to the designs from one of their esteemed clients.

Her team of around 12 members went to the cafe close by. The waiter joined the tables in the garden area for them to sit together. Arannya was not close to anyone except Gwen. She was her office bestie, as they shared common haters.

"Gwen, can we skip this and go get a beer?" Arannya asked.

"Aarna, there's no escape, as Eshani is also joining," informed Gwen.

Eshani was the firm's co-director.

"What! Why is she coming?" Arannya smirked; she disliked Eshani's haughty behaviour with employees.

The tea and cookies arrived as people started to chit-chat about other companies and the clients they have acquired lately. Gwen and Arannya, seated at the corner, were enjoying their tea and snacks. They have already finished one round of Arannya's favourite quesadilla.

Suddenly everyone stood up as Eshani arrived. Arannya was the last one to stand up.

"Hi Aarna, hello everyone," Eshani deliberately took her name to make sure she listens and responds to her. Arannya returned it with a fake smile.

"First of all, great job, guys; the designs were all so well done, they got approved with negligible feedback, and we can expect more work from the recommendations!" announced Eshani, and everyone clapped.

"As the work was excellent, our client wanted to come in person and thank all of us. They will be here at any moment."

Two extra chairs were placed at the corner for them, right next to Arannya. After a while, two men came and greeted everyone. Mr. Harish came along with his son.

"So is this the talented team behind those amazing designs?" Mr. Harish smiled and nodded hello to everyone. "Please enjoy the snacks. The food is on us." Saying so, both he and his son sat on the chair placed for them.

"Stingy ares," Arannya cursed and saw the son who was sitting next to her from the corner of her eye. It seemed to her that he heard what she said.

Arannya nudged Gwen to leave but got silenced in return. To avoid the boring meeting, she opened her Pinterest and started scrolling. She saw that Zavian texted her, but she decided to open that app once she was back home.

20 minutes later, everyone stood up to leave. Arannya, who was busy on her phone, got up and tried to fetch a glass of water for herself, but accidentally the glass slipped and the water spilt on the client. She was too embarrassed to even look at the person, so she dug her eyes to the ground and apologised. "I am extremely sorry, sir." She took her bag, bit her lips, and left from there. Gwen went right after her.

"It's alright," the son said to Eshani, asking her to tell Arannya not to worry so much, and he giggled.

Arannya took an autorickshaw to her flat. It's 10 past 8, and she was full. To kill time, she put on a web series on her laptop and started scrolling through her Pinterest account. She got a text from Zavian.

She opened the app, and there were about 10 unread messages from him.

"Hello? Are you there?"

"Hey, what happened?"

"I am sorry if I offended you in any way."

"At least reply."

"Hii Alizehhhh"

"Thanks for making me believe in my fate. Love is not meant for me."

"Alright, I give up, Dasvidaniya Al," with a crying emoji.

Arannya suddenly got reminded of Kartik when she read Dasvidaniya.

This intrigued her to text back, "Hii."

"Thank God," she got an instant reply.

"I thought you got offended." Zavian texted.

"Not really," she replied with a smile.

They chatted about various things and also confessed about their forged online identity, their likes and dislikes, what they do, and where they work. Zavian was working in an IT company, and Arannya said she is a student of philosophy. After talking about random things, Zavian asked if they could meet up that night. Arannya went offline right after he asked her out.

'Whenever–wherever we're meant to be together.' The doorbell rang. It was Shiba.

"Hi Aaru, haven't you cooked anything to eat? I'm famished!" Shiba exaggerated and threw herself on the bed.

"Sorry, Shiba, I'm full; please order something." Arannya said as she was scrolling something on her phone.

"Okay, fine! Anyway, tell me, did you order someone from the dating app?" Shiba mocked.

"Shiba!!! Actually, yes." Arannya replied.

"What!" Shiba screamed with excitement.

Arannya told her about the conversations with Zavian and how she was feeling anxious.

Shiba gave a light knock on her head and started searching the wardrobe to find an outfit for her.

"Hold on, I did not say yes, and I don't know if he will be back online, even if I text him now."

"Leave that to me and go get ready." Saying so, Shiba pushed her to the washroom.

While Aarna was freshening up, Shiba texted Zavian and got an instant reply. He has asked Alizeh to come to Moonlight Sky Lounge at 10 sharp. Shiba texted him that she'll be wearing a silver top to help identify her easily. She pulled out her silver off-shoulder top and gave it to Arannya.

"Alizeh! Here, since you are nonchalant about wearing a dress, at least wear this top, and yes, it's non-negotiable, honey." Shibha winked and left the room for her to change.

"Don't call me Alizeh!!" Arannya murmured and got ready.

"Who is Alizeh?" Fatima came out of her room after offering her Namaz and asked.

"I'll explain everything to you over dinner, Fatti; tell me what you want to eat. I'm ordering, and you don't forget to wear my perfume for extra effect," Shiba said to both Fatima and Arannya, respectively.

After the disapproval about her tied hair from Shiba, she kept her hair open and applied a dark shade of lipstick, which was not her style, but she couldn't argue with her as it was already half past nine, and the cab was on its way.

Arannya was shy and, in fact, awkward about this whole situation. But Shiba's pep talk helped her to curb her scepticism.

Arannya, alias Alizeh, got into the cab and shared the OTP number.

"It's an incorrect OTP, ma'am," the driver said.

"It's correct."

"Madam, you are sharing my car number," he said.

Aarna bit her lips and gave him the correct OTP this time.

While in the cab, she opened her compact powder and checked her face; surprisingly, the dark lipstick is actually looking good on her. Her hands were sweating, and she was getting anxious. What if someone sees her? What if he turns out to be a thief or a scammer? As instructed by Shiba, she has shared her live location with her. But all these negative thoughts flooded her mind, and she was about to ask the driver to take her back to the pickup point. But then her phone chimed, "Hi Alizeh. I have reached the destination; come towards the right side of the bar counter. I am wearing a black shirt."

"Alright." She replied.

She knew going back would not be a great idea as Shiba would kill her; hence she decided she would go have a mocktail and leave, simple. Yes, that's more gracious, she said to herself.

She got down from the cab and went inside the complex to take the lift to the 7th floor.

In the lift on the 3rd floor, there was a restaurant named Kartik Foods. She closed her eyes and thought of Kartik. "I'm sorry, Kartik," she murmured as she felt guilty.

"Right side from the bar, black shirt," she said softly as she struggled to find Zavian. Since all the waiters were also wearing black shirts, she got totally confused. She stood on the left corner of the bar and was tapping her phone on her lips while scanning each and every table carefully. Finally, she saw a person who was sitting facing towards the only lake in the city. His back was facing towards her.

She walked to the table, and upon seeing her, he stood up.

"Oh hi! Such a funny coincidence." The man said.

For a moment, she froze, as if someone had chopped her tongue. She couldn't believe the irony of her fate; forget about saying hi; she turned to leave at once! The person was none other than Mr. Harish's son.

"Please have a seat," he insisted.

Arannya gathered some courage to face this predicament. He pulled the chair for her, and she sat.

"Hi," she replied, while trying to look away from him and acting as if she was searching for some known face in that crowd.

"Hey, look, if I am making you feel uncomfortable, I can leave; don't worry. But if it is about the incident in the cafe, then I guess you should just chill about it. Let's start from the start, as I know your name is definitely not Alizeh, right, Arannya?" he asked.

"Yeah, right, and you are?"

"I'm Karan, not Zavian," he smiled.

"I'm sorry, Karan; actually, this is the first time I've come to meet someone like this, so I'm a bit awkward about the whole thing. All I wanted to ask is, just keep it to yourself; don't mention it to Eshani; I know you guys are family friends."

"Excuse me, take the order, please." He called the waiter, ignoring what she said. Arannya was baffled.

"Get me a cognac with tonic water and a chill pill for Umm Alizeh," he said and winked at her.

"Cognac will do," said Arannya; she started to get comfortable.

Sipping on their drinks, they talked about the place, the increasing traffic in the city, and how the weather is too hot for September. But mostly they talked about the one thing common between them, their work. Karan told her he has recently returned from Australia and is emotionally blackmailed into joining his dad's business. After another round of cognac and a plate of chicken nachos. They decided to leave.

"Funny how our supposed 'date' turned out to be a business meeting." Karan said as they came out of the lift to the ground floor.

"Agreed!" said Arannya.

"But have you noticed one thing?" Asked Karan.

"What?"

"Our Aliases sound phonetic. Alizeh-Zavian" he chuckled.

"Where do you stay? I will give you a ride." Karan offered.

"No, please don't bother; my cab will be here in a minute. Oh, there it is!" She pointed to a grey-coloured hatchback. "That was quick!" He said as she walked towards the cab. She did not hear this, though.

"Good night." Arannya said and got inside the cab.

"Good night," Karan replied. "Drive her safe," he requested of the driver.

As soon as she arrived, Shiba was excited to know how it went while she herself was getting ready for her date. Shiba's parties usually start at midnight.

"So, did you guys kiss? Was he hot?" Shiba shot her questions, "Wait, Shiba, let me take a piss first!" Arannya said and ran to the washroom.

"You got a text from your date, Aaru." Shiba shouted from outside for her to hear inside the washroom. She was blushing.

She applied extra pressure to empty the bladder at the earliest and buttoned up her jeans. She even forgot to zip her pants, rushed out of the washroom, and pounced on her phone.

"Look at her! Already head over heels for..." Shiba took a pause. "What's his real name, by the way?"

"Zavian! Sorry, Karan, it's Karan" saying that she went straight to the app's messenger and texted back, "Hi, yes, I reached safely; I hope you did too." After waiting for eleven minutes, she thought maybe Karan had just been humble enough and not really bothered about this meeting. Not to look too inclined, she texted, "Good night," leaving no chance for more conversation.

Arannya turned her mobile data off and went to sleep. She had a subtle blush on her face this time. She was amused over what happened, and she couldn't wait to tell Gwen about this the next morning.

It was an unusually early morning for Arannya; her eyes opened around 5:38 am before her alarm, which was two hours early to her sleep schedule. But even with a premature sleep, she felt like she had a wonderful sleep at night.

"Yes, I did! It was nice knowing you, Aarna. Good night!" As soon as she woke up, she read this text from Karan on Flechazo.

She reached the office before time today; only the office boy Chandu was there. "Good morning, Didi, *aaj jaldi aa gaye*! Should I get tea for you?" he asked. "Nahi Bhaiya, Badmein."

She then checked her emails, went through some designs she had to evaluate, and kept the sticky notes with the most important follow-ups on her monitor.

After 30 minutes, the office started to fill in, and she couldn't wait and dialled Gwen, "Gwen! Where are you?"

"I'm on the way, Aaru; what happened?"

"Nothing, just come soon."

"Yeah, give me 10."

The moment Gwen arrived, Arannya took their coffee mugs and literally dragged Gwen along with her to the cafeteria.

"Aaru! What's happening? What's the gossip? Anything about Eshani?" Huffing and puffing, Gwen bombarded her questions.

"Guess what!" She began and told her all that happened last night.

Having the first sip of hot coffee, Gwen got her tongue burnt. "Tch, are you an idiot? Who will say no to a ride in a Porsche and choose a taxi over it? Are you really that dumb?" This was the takeaway for Arannya from the conversation.

It was a lazy afternoon that day; she and Gwen had chole bhature, and all she could think about was sleep. Around 3 pm, she asked Gwen if she wanted to have some coffee. Gwen rejected the offer as she was working on that month's balance sheet for the CA. Arannya was unable to control her sleep, so she grabbed a mug for her. As she walked out of the cafeteria door, she bumped into someone and spilled a considerable amount of coffee on his shirt; the drops made their way to his shoe.

"Shit! I am extremely sorry." Without looking up, she apologised to the person.

"No, you are not!" A similar voice rang in her ears.

Seeing Arannya's face turn black and blue, Gwen raised her eyebrows, questioning her state. Arannya rolled her eyes at Karan, who was walking toward Eshanis Cabin.

Duh duh duh duh She could hear her heartbeat clearly.

'Trung trung' rang the phone at her desktop. "Yes," she said in a very low voice.

"Aarna, please come to my cabin." That was Eshani.

The 10-second walk from her desk to Eshani's cabin was one of the scariest for her; her mind clouded with all sorts of negative thoughts. She was hating her decision to go on that app and listen to Shiba. What might Karan have told Eshani? She was convinced she would definitely lose her dignity, if not her job.

'*Knock knock,*' she entered her cabin. Keeping her posture as calm as she could, she looked straight at Eshani, completely ignoring Karan's presence there. Eshani explained that Karan needs a few design changes in his office, and since Deepak is on a two-week leave, she wants her to take the lead on this.

Arannya could listen to nothing but some words, which made no sense to her at that point in time. "Aarna, Aarna! Do you follow?" Eshani nudged her and got her back to the present.

"Yes, Eshani," she replied vaguely. "Great, then! Take Karan to the studio room, and I will join in a while." said Eshani.

"Sorry?" Arannya questioned.

"Aarna, smell some coffee and wake up already!" Eshani taunted.

"Shall we?" gestured Karan by swinging his hand towards the door.

Arannya was in a tight spot, and she was hating the decision to go on a blind date.

They came inside the studio room; all the raw materials—crafts, wooden pieces, sheets of wooden design, etc.—were piled up in one corner. "Are you really here for work?" she asked.

"What do you think?" giggled Karan.

"I'm scared; this is my workplace."

"But why? I'm here for work," he smiled.

She gave him a stern look; her heart was beating abnormally.

"Or, have I startled you because you've been thinking of me this morning and I showed up, correct?"

"What! No!!!" Arannya tried hard to deny what he said, but being bad at hiding what was inside her heart, her expression said it all. This was her weakness. Wearing her heart upon her sleeve has put her in embarrassing positions more often than not.

Eshani came inside and asked if Karan briefed her about the changes he wished to make.

Arannya said yes, but she had to do the reiki to design the walk-in closet that Karan wanted inside his office. Arannya was very sincere when it came to work. So she started right at it.

Karan asked if this could be done with a little priority, and Eshani assigned the task to Arannya immediately.

"Aarna, you fill in for Deepak here, and I will ask him to evaluate the playschool design you were working on. I hope that shouldn't be an issue!" Said Eshani as she browsed something on her phone.

Arannya had no choice but to nod a yes.

"Great! Let's start then." Said Karan euphorically.

"Now?" asked Arannya.

"Yes, because I don't want to waste even a minute more." Giggled Karan, and this caught Eshani's eye. She chose to feign ignorance.

Arannya went to her desk to get some measuring instruments and her bag. Gwen, who was watching this quietly, finally spoke, "Are you going to tell me now, or do I have to wait?"

"Later," she answered and went off.

Arannya's heart began to beat abnormally; she was anxious. Karan came and stood next to her; they were waiting for the lift. The lift arrived with a space left only for these two.

They had to stand very close to each other, and as they reached the ground floor, people started to rush out of the lift, pushing them closer.

Her heart was racing.

Karan signalled the valet to get his car. After a few minutes, the white Porsche came, and Karan opened the door for her. How chivalrous she thought.

For someone like him, who belonged to one of the richest families in town, being handsome was an inherent trait. It was a 20-minute drive to Karan's office. The infotainment screen showed the last song played by Karan was 'Oh Meri Jaan' from Life in Metro. Karan asked if she wanted to play something of her choice; she said, "That's my choice," and they got engrossed in the refreshing music.

'Dil khudgarz hai, phisla hai yeh phir haath se.

Kal, uska raha, ab hai tera, iss raat se...'

And then the YouTube algorithm did its best to play all the soulful songs following that.

They reached his office; he gave car keys to the driver, and they went to the lift; his office was on the 7th floor. All the construction noise could be heard as it was a new building. They came to the 7th floor; the tile work was done; there were plywoods, frames, saws, and boxes of adhesive around; the workers had not arrived yet.

"So, this is what Deepak has designed for the office, but I need the closet in my cabin." Karan said.

"Why are you so fixated on having a closet, though?" Said Arannya as she was checking out his office space and how and where she could plan for that. She was curious.

"Umm, you see, there are times when people can spill things on my shirt, and I can just go for a quick rescue in my closet. Hahaha." He laughed.

Arannya looked at him sharply from the corner of her eyes. "Killer!" Karan mouthed at her from across the other corner of the room.

"Okay, so if we keep the closet here, we need to lose the window because this is where the closet can fit best. But I think we can keep the window inside the walk-in wardrobe; let me see," she said as she went to take the measuring tape from her bag and her notepad.

"Could you please come and help here?" She said as she opened the roll meter and pointed to Karan.

Karan pushed the tape back with his palm and came close to her. So close that she could feel his breath on her ear. She froze. As much as she knew the right thing to do was push him away or back off, she didn't. He planted a kiss exactly between her left earlobe and cheek, making her aroused instantly. He then intertwined his right hand with her left, and she held it back. The grip was hot, strong, and sweaty.

"Look at me," Karan whispered in her ear. She lifted her chin up and saw straight into his eyes; they were brownish grey, but his eyelashes were perfectly curled up as if he'd applied mascara.

She slides her vision from left to right and down at his lips. He bent a little to reach her lips and kissed her. She showed a little resistance. Karan tried to kiss her again, and this time she couldn't resist and kissed him back. It was a fiery kiss; they could both feel the heat in their mouths. She never tasted something so delicious. And both of them dove into a session of passionate kissing for the next ten minutes.

'Please close the door, kripya darwaja band kare.' The lift alarmed them, and they came back to their senses.

It was the workers. They greeted Karan and went to change their clothes in a temporary room with tents that they made. She could see the lady giggling.

"This is embarrassing; why is she giggling? Did they get to know what we were doing?"

"Definitely, as I ate all your lipstick."

"Shit!" she exclaimed in embarrassment and took lipstick out of her purse for a retouch.

She did some measurements of his office and instructed the workers. After 45 minutes, she asked for her leave. Karan offered to drop, and she agreed.

On the journey back to her office, they did not say anything, but the energy between them was nothing less than an exothermic reaction.

As they reached near her office, Karan held her hand and said, "You can trust me." Arannya saw him with her eyes full of hope.

This was just the beginning of the torrid romance they were going to indulge in. Arannya, having been single all her prime years, fell for him instantly; she felt as if her fate pitied her after all.

This was the moment she wore those rose-coloured glasses.

The fire between them was incredible, and they quickly bonded and surrendered to each other. The spark between them grew brighter; they were living a love song.

Arannya finally got all she could ever ask for. Her world was filled with love and happiness. Karan made her feel heard and seen. His visits to her office increased exponentially, making every eyebrow raise with curiosity to find out what's cooking.

Arannya started to live in a fantasy world that Karan has created around her.

He started to take her out for lunch every afternoon; if on days when he was busy he'd order lunch for her, he'd pick her up from her office and drop her off on the days if they had taken any trips or stayed together the previous night. Usually Karan would take her to his farmhouse, which was on the outskirts of the city, and return the next morning.

One afternoon he visited her office to meet Eshani. He was holding two cups of coffee; he kept one at her desk while she was engrossed in her work. She saw the cup had his name written on it. When she looked at him, he turned the cup he was holding, and it had her name on it. She blushed, he winked, and her cheeks went pink.

He made her life no less than a fairy tale. She became delusional. She was so engrossed in her life that she didn't realise when she made distance with Gwen.

Her world began to revolve around Karan. She started to deck up every single day for him, looked for the lucky colour of the day in the horoscope and wore those colours, changed the way she smelt, and invested a large amount of her salary in luxe items.

Since Karan belonged to one of the blue-eyed families, they instantly became the talk of the town. For the next 6 months, they explored every beautiful cafe, club, and pub. But the City Folks Club was the most elite club of all, and only the VIPs would get the membership. Karan's family wasn't an exception here.

Arannya became the default plus one with Karan. Every party he was invited to, she accompanied him.

She has enhanced her dress sense and the way she interacted with people.

In one of the parties they got clicked together, Arnanya is laughing, and Karan is looking at her with dewy eyes. This photograph made its way to the local tabloid. Under the heading of "Cupid struck," with some other couples, but their picture took the largest space in that article. Arannya was lovestruck and high on fame. She was unapologetically enjoying all the attention she was garnering. When a person gets something he is convinced he'd never have, it can make him go nuts and feel over the top. Only a few managed to be grounded.

Arannya was so intoxicated with this sudden dynamic change in her life that the lines between logic and fantasy blurred. She became snobbish towards Shiba and Fatima too. With gaining popularity in social circles, she was riding on high horses.

Having found a person like Karan, who treated her like a trophy and spoiled her with gifts and surprises, nothing could ever go wrong, she was convinced. And when the lesser mortals feel like nothing can go wrong, there comes a blow out of nowhere and trashes them on the ground, making them realise their place.

In one of the parties, Eshani questioned her, "Are you guys serious about each other?"

"Of course we are!" Arannya almost exclaimed. There was arrogance in her tone. And when arrogance takes over a person, they should be prepared for the downfall. Hers was just around the corner.

That night Arannya tried her best to keep an imposter face throughout the party, but Eshani's question shook her from inside. The doubt started to creep into her heart; she might even have felt these before but never paid any attention to these feelings, fearing, "What if it's true?" Karan, on the other hand, never did or said anything for her to get sceptical, but a woman's heart knows the things that are unexpressed.

In fact, they never conversed about where this relationship was going. It all started with one conversation and Shiba pushing her in the field of casual dating, but Arannya should have known better that this lane was not for her. She is not made for casual things but exclusivity. Though Shiba kept a check on her in between and gave her a reality check only to date for fun and romance and not to get serious, she foolishly fell in love yet again.

One day after a steamy lovemaking session, Arannya gathered the courage and asked him the difficult question.

"Karan, do you love me?"

"Of course, baby, what kind of question is that?"

"Then tell me, what is the next step?" She hinted at marriage.

"Look me in the eye. Tell me what you see." Karan sang.

"Deep within a drowning of me," she added, and they hugged. Eshani is jealous, she concluded.

Karan kissed her forehead and hugged her tightly, but he did not answer her question. She thought of letting that slide and clung on to the hug, thinking maybe he is not ready just yet. But she could sense a mayhem. Intuitions are for real.

The next day, Arannya received a message from Karan informing her that he had left for Singapore for some urgent work and that he wouldn't be available for the next two weeks.

She tried calling him, but his phone was switched off. She got worried. How can he just drop a text and leave? He could at least meet her or call her. She called his friends; nobody had an answer; she called his office; nobody knew anything. She called Eshani, and she hung up on her, saying she was driving, and asked her to meet in the office. She got ready in a jiffy and landed straight at her cabin.

"Eshani, do you have any updates about Karan?"

"Well, I should be the one asking this question." Eshani passed a cunning smile.

"Eshani, not now, please. I am so worried. Please help me." Arannya's arrogant tone shifted to that of a criminal who, after pleading guilty, was begging for a lenient punishment.

Eshani said she doesn't have any clue and that she will have to wait until he returns.

This period of exile was like walking on burning coals for Arannya. She had all the bad thoughts; she hated why she let the question asked by Eshani bother her; she shouldn't have asked the question.

Every day she texted him, but the messages wouldn't go through. She attempted calling him even when his phone was switched off, hoping he'd turn it on and she could get through. She went crazy, had a loss of appetite, and didn't go to work. That made it worse; Fatima and Shiba encouraged her to keep herself busy and out of her character; Shiba consoled her the most. She took her to a party, drank beer with her, and listened to all her cribbing and sob stories. Shiba was really concerned about her.

It was like Karan asked Arannya to jump off the cliff, promising he would catch her, but he just pushed her to the depths of the chasm. She understood one thing about herself: that she is a fragile person, and more than that, an imbecile. How many times can she possibly fall in love and get her heart broken? There has to be an end to this. Enough is enough, she thought. Even after knowing that she isn't the chosen one to experience true love, she keeps challenging her destiny and takes fatal and failed chances with her heart.

History seemed to repeat, and she became weaker and weaker. It was like she didn't know herself anymore. But still, her foolish heart prayed for a miracle that things should just be fine between her and Karan. Hope was like a thin thread she was clinging to.

Listening to Shiba, she went to the office after a week.

"Good morning, ma'am. Chai?" Asked Chandu. She nodded.

She went to Gwen and hugged her and was about to break down, but Gwen consoled her that it's okay, and they will go to someplace after work.

"Hi Aarna, How have you been?" asked Deepak. He was holding certain folders in his hands.

"I am good, Deepak, thank you," she said. "How is the Mayflower project going?"

"Almost done; need to get consent on some final add-ons and touch-ups. I will get it done once Karan sir is in today."

"What do you mean by 'today'? "Is he back in town?" she asked.

"Yes! It's been three days," he replied.

Arannya dashed into Eshani's cabin. Let me take up the Mayflower. She said, and Eshani replied it's a closed project now, and Deepak is already on it. Arannya knew that Eshani had all the information about Karan. Since she was her employer, she couldn't question her. She clenched her fists and rushed out of the cabin.

"Don't do anything stupid," Eshanis's voice volumed out, reaching her ears but not brain.

"Hi Deepak! Actually, I have to go towards that area for a new project, Reiki. I wouldn't mind getting a few signs for you." Arannya maintained a very normal posture with a smile.

Who in the world would not like to get their work done without asking for it? Deepak agreed instantly, as she had also handled this client in his absence.

As soon as Deepak gave her the folder, she picked up her bag and ran out of the office.

She hired a taxi and agreed on whatever amount the driver asked for the trip. "Please drive fast, Dada," she requested.

Now there were thousands of questions running through her mind—what she would do next and how she was going to confront him. What was the reason that he just went MIA on her? She thought about her poor state of self in the past few days and hated it. Anger started to fill her heart, and at a point she thought of stopping the taxi and going back. She clenched her teeth, as if she was attempting to break her jaw. She closed her eyes and thought of all the beautiful moments with Karan. Tears started to roll; she knew this was a make-it-or break it meeting; she could sense it was already over, but she still hung on to this funny thing called 'hope.'

All her inhibitions and frustration were surpassed by the emotion of her getting to see him, meet him, and feel him. And she was convinced that one hug would melt him in her arms. Just like he used to claim!

"Madam, are you okay?" asked the curious driver.

"No, Bhaiya, but I will be." She wiped her tears as she said this and smiled politely.

"Don't worry, Madam; you seem to be a good person. God will do what's best. At times we feel, Why is God not giving us what we want so badly? But he will always make the plans fail that are not meant for us, and in the end you will find yourself in a perfectly happy place. Believe me, madam, in the end everything will be good. Just like our cinemas."

Arannya heard the sermon from the driver as if some divine entity came inside him to convey this to her.

She reached, paid him in cash, and asked to keep the change. "Thank you, Madam. Everything is going to be alright." He said and drove off.

Arannya went near the lift; it was on the fourth floor. She couldn't waste a minute and took the stairs.

Panting and trying to catch her breath, she reached the seventh floor. The office setup was almost through, and the final touch-ups were going on.

"Hi Bhaiya, is Karan Sir there?"

The security guard's face turned yellow; he didn't say a word as if he was tongue-tied.

He looked towards his cabin, where he was. Arannya rushed inside his cabin and saw he was speaking to a lady who was sitting on the chair opposite to him.

"Oh! Hi!" The lady turned towards Arannya and greeted her.

"A little knocking would have been considerate," the lady said and turned towards Karan. Karan was standing numb. His blood went dry.

"Apologies, but I need some urgent sign-offs from Mr. Karan." Arannya held her frustration, but the undercurrents were clearly felt.

"Alright. You guys carry on, and I will see you at dinner," said the lady to Karan as she lifted her bag.

Arannya did not notice the girl, but her henna smelt too strong to go unnoticed.

Karan accompanied the lady to the lift, and Arannya saw they hugged. This was a very general gesture for Karan to do; she held her storm.

As soon as he came inside, she hugged him. She hugged him tight, as if she would lose him if she left him at that moment.

"I'm sorry, Aarna," Karan apologised in a trembling voice.

"Don't be sorry, Baby, it's okay. Now that you are back, I don't have any complaints about you. Only one request: whenever you have to leave like this, just keep me updated. That's it."

She noticed he wasn't holding her back. She held his hands and tried to wrap them around her waist. Karan was reluctant. "Baby, hold me properly." As she touched his hands again, she felt a ring on his finger.

She detached herself within a second. Took his hand to confirm what she had felt.

There it was. A platinum band on his ring finger made it clear that he got engaged.

She fell on the ground, her eyes fixed on the floor. How could he, how could he, she was murmuring. As if the blood inside her body ran cold, her breath stopped; even her eyes were so heavy that she was unable to blink. She was breathing slowly.

"Aarna, let me explain everything that happened..." Arannya couldn't hear a word of what he was saying; she couldn't comprehend the situation. How exactly she got into this mess. Was she too blind to not see, or did she choose to be blind and let it go for however much the life of this relationship was? She wondered.

Karan tried to lift her up. "Get up, Aarna."

"Don't touch me!" She struggled a bit to get up on her own, took the folder and her bag, and without saying another word, left from there.

That's it.

She couldn't feel her heart, as if it died in that cabin. She did not wait for the lift but took the stairs; she didn't want anyone to notice her. As if she has committed a crime, hasn't she? She committed a crime towards her heart. Once bitten and thrice shy.

She came down and saw the same taxi driver. Was it a coincidence, or was he deliberately waiting for her?

"Bhaiya, is it vacant?" She asked.

"Where should I drop you, Madam?" He questioned back.

She asked him to just keep on driving and not to stop. He obliged. He drove her through the city; her phone kept ringing; people from the office were calling her; she didn't care. She switched her phone off after some time. She leaned on the window and kept looking outside with an empty gaze and no thoughts. She didn't want to think about anything, not even her current state of where she is right now. Just zero thoughts in her mind. It kept raining from the clouds and from her eyes continuously, and he kept driving.

It was almost late evening, and night started to take over when the driver finally asked, "Madam, this is the third time we are crossing the same place; I think you should go home now, Madam." He was now concerned.

"Where do you want me to drop you?" He asked again.

Arannya didn't say anything. So the driver dropped her near her office from where he picked her up.

To his surprise, she took 4k from her wallet and gave it to him. "Madam, this?" The driver had mixed emotions at that time. He was surprised, confused, and sad at her state but happy for the trip amount he received.

"Thank you," she said and left.

She went to the office and asked the watchman to open the office for her.

Everyone had left by this time. She felt relieved that she could sob in peace. In the studio room where different props and materials were kept; at times, some carpentry classes would also take place there. Due to this reason, that room was soundproof.

She went inside, locked the room, and clenched her top, sat on the floor, and cried out loud; she shouted at the top of her lungs and cried. She cried thinking about how stupid she could be to even think of a future with him; such things happen in novels and movies, not in reality. She is jinxed in the matter of love. How dare she think she'll succeed! She cried for making a fool out of herself. She could feel her stomach getting sucked in due to the unbearable pain in her heart. She felt and in fact wished that she could die at that moment. As she tried harder to close her eyes, she saw Dadu's face.

Remembered all the moments with him and how he used to treat her like a princess. And if only he had been alive, he would have burnt the world before the tear would drop from her eyes. His words echoed in her ears, *"Then darling, you be that person."*

She felt hopeless and directionless. She pulled her hair in anger; she was angry at herself but was disgusted over Karan. She considered him as her soul mate, the best person ever, that one special one who was made for her, but in the end he was just another ordinary man.

It was her who made him special; otherwise, he was just another ordinary man.

She wept until all the pain in her soul was out in the form of tears. This incident did not break her heart, but it broke her soul. And this was a sin she committed towards herself.

That night she literally begged God to give her strength to overcome this and take the feelings for Karan away.

And it happened too eventually, but it was a long war up the hill.

After that night, Arannya never went back to the office; she left the city and moved back to her parents. Her parents knew something was wrong. But they never nudged her; they knew it was a heartbreak, and they hoped that she would get over it. Arannya had a very generic relationship with her parents; she needed something, she would ask, and they would give it to her. She always got what she demanded, but in the case of her relationships, it never worked out.

There is a saying in Urdu: *"Kabhi kisi ko mukammal jahan nahi milta, kisi ko zameen to kisi ko aasmaan nahi milta."*

Which means, "Never in life would it happen that one would get everything; some may not get the ground, and some may not get the skies." So isn't life a constant pull between these two? A delusion that one has everything while in fact it's just that the pull is stronger on one side, and it may lose to gravity anytime?

She indeed was old school; the connection she nurtured with Karan was with a hope of taking it to its final destination, but she still had to learn a very harsh truth about love. Love is nothing but a losing game; you either lose your heart or the person; in the end, you'll be a loser.

She believed that the fleeting connection was her forever. How old was her soul in this new world?

And yet again she was left *hopeless.*

The Metamorphosis

When a person lives a life where his beliefs have been questioned, luck has been tested, faith has been broken, and hopes have been shattered, he goes into a phase of forced internal transformation, not cursory but at the core level. Every experience turns into a lesson, reshaping him into a whole new person. Furthermore, reflecting the change in the visage and physiognomy in a similar fashion as ecdysis.

This is the phase of metamorphosis. Remember the times when you hated a particular thing and happened to like it over time? It could be anything: a person, a thing, a ritual, a song, or a place. People commonly call this phenomenon 'maturity.'

The sense of realisation that our existence is of such less significance and that we may not be as important to this world as we think instills a sense of gratitude in us. Nonetheless, we are important to the world within, aren't we?

Even without luck, faith, hope, and love, we continue to live our journey, constantly reminding ourselves that we are enough.

But, Are we really enough?

The past experiences made Arannya grow into a sensible, logical, practical, and diplomatic girl who fits in the world seamlessly. Her soft heart and inner child were long lost, and for the better.

She moved to a mega tech city and stayed in an apartment with another roommate who was working as an assistant DOP in regional TV dramas. Her name was Sri Laxmi. But she would kill if anyone called her by that name; her alias was 'Lax.' She had a very eccentric personality, full of life, very positive; wherever she went, she used to carry that positive aura with her. She was 3 years younger than Arannya, and her enthusiasm always inspired her. Though Arannya became structured now, she loved to be around Laxmi; Laxmi used to address Arannya as *Akka*, which is sister in Telugu.

The owners of the flat were an old couple who were staying two lanes beside their flat. They were happy with these girls, as Arannya never got any of her friends or colleagues to her flat, and Lax, even when she got her friends, they were very well behaved, and few of them were working in some famous TV serials, which made the owners boast about this to their neighbours and relatives. They had such cordial relations with the owners that in two years they did not increase the rent even.

It was 9 pm on a Sunday when Arannya came home with a sullen face. Lax was watching some series on TV and munching on popcorn.

"Surprise!" Lax said. Usually Lax wouldn't be home around this time.

"What happened? No shoot or party for you tonight?" asked Arannya.

"Forget about me, Akka. Tell me, how was your date?" Lax's pupil grew bigger as she asked this to Arannya.

"Don't ask; it's not going to work." Said answered as she grabbed some popcorn from her bowl and sat next to her.

"What was the deal breaker?" Lax handed over the bowl to Arannya and turned towards her and sat in a Burmese pose.

"So, the turn down was, he said he had a great sex life, and he was looking for someone with a similar background." Arannya made a duck face, and they both laughed.

"Then it's impossible, because you and sex life are a concept yet to be discovered by this world, hahah," Lax laughed.

Arannya just smiled politely. After Karan, she completely shut her feelings down, turning herself asexual. Even if she tells about her past to Lax, she would never believe it, because she has known her for two years, and there wasn't a single person Arannya talked about or even dated.

This was her life now: get up, go for the morning walk, come back, cook breakfast for both of them, go to work, take two coffee breaks and one lunch break, while coming back pick some groceries at times, ask Lax if she will be eating at home, go home, pour some wine for herself, put on some music, and cook. Now this was her treasured time of the day, where she was alone at home, sipping her favourite wine and cooking. This was her therapy. Talk to Mom and Dad like a daily ritual, tell them what she made, ask them what they were eating, check profiles of the boys her Mom would send, and fix the meet on weekends, usually Sundays.

Arannya was not really ready for the marriage; she thought every other man in this world would deceive her like her past experiences. Even though she pretended to be fine, deep down the cut was still fresh.

Since her parents were getting old, she compromised on the fact that she could be a happy single and started to show genuine interest in finding a partner through all the profiles her mom would send her.

It's been almost a year now, but nothing ever went to the stage of marriage, only meeting, getting to know, and then eventually it'll fizzle out.

Many times the reason was she herself. On most of the dates she just zoned out and ended up giving off vibes to the other person, which led them to misjudge her about her interest in the institution called marriage.

Apart from this, she found peace within herself; she was earning a handsome amount where she did not have to be dependent on her parents' money. She used to take solo trips within her country and go on group trips internationally on strict guidelines from her mother.

She never felt the need of having a man's love now. She was convinced that she had seen it all, and she is not among the special people who will find and keep love.

In her life she was always blessed with good fortune when it came to money. And cursed when it came to love.

There was a person, though, who was head over heels for Arannya. He was a supporting actor in a regional TV serial and a friend to Lax. Though being a supporting actor, he's surprisingly gained more popularity than the main character of his serial. All credit goes to his good looks.

His name was Gautam. He never used to miss any opportunity when Lax used to invite her friends over. Arannya used to give them company at times, not that she loved it, but just to keep Lax's heart. That doesn't mean she did not enjoy it, but after some point in time, she used to zone out and go back to her room. She didn't want to be a spoilsport after all. But always ended up being one.

One such night, everyone gathered at their apartment, except for Gautam. He was busy with his late-night shoot and was supposed to join them afterwards.

Arannya did not feel like drinking since it was a Sunday and she had her office the next day.

Lax's phone rang; it was Gautam.

Yes, "Goo," that's what Lax used to address him as.

"Yeah, yeah, fine, sorry! Tell me, have you started?"

"What! Pick a cab and come, bro!"

"Everyone is sloshed over here."

While saying this, Lax saw Arannya, who was busy eating the soya kabab.

"No, wait, tell me where you are. I will send someone to pick you up."

Arannya had no clue she would ask her to go fetch him, "Akka, please, Akka, he has a lot of gossip to share today. Please pick him up for us." Along with Lax, her other friends Chaitra, Emraan, Daniel, and Rishi also started to literally beg her.

Arannya gave in to their pleading and agreed to pick him up. Emraan asked her to take his car, but she took her own since she knows how to drive only an automatic car.

She reached the place and saw a guy wearing this black hoodie when it's not even winter. He made a stiff wave from his hand, and she stopped near him. As per his usual habit, he started to blabber as soon as he got in the car, "Thank you very, very, very much, Master."

"Don't call me that," she said.

"Mam would not suit you, and since I've decided to surrender to you, you are my master." He said and giggled and pulled out a wedelia from his pocket. "Accept it, Master, just a little thank-you gesture." He winked and buckled the seat belt. "Just Aarna, please." She said and drove off.

"And come out of your character; there are no cameras here." Arannya giggled. She loved the gesture, though.

This wasn't the first time Gautam had made such gestures; even in fun, it was evident that he had a liking towards Arannya. But Arannya was phobic to this feeling now; she was unmoved.

There were moments when, if Arannya needed water, he would be swift enough to get up and get the bottle for her. And the friends used to hoot and make funny gestures; Aarnaya also used to smile and blush, but she never had anything in her heart for him. She was simply playing along.

There was a time when she got a charley horse in her legs and he quickly came to her rescue and gave her a massage. It really gave her a relief, but she got awkward and asked to take her leave from the party and went to her room. People got to know that was awkward, but Gautam just shrugged it off and made another peg for himself.

In one of the truth and dare games, Gautam got the dare of praising Aarnaya; Emraan gave him the dare, but it was as if this was planned earlier.

Arannya was unbothered.

"Uhh, ehhh." Gautam cleared his throat.

"But for this I would like to hold the hand of the lady I am going to praise," he announced.

"Oh ho ho, go Gautam! Tonight is the night to say what you feel. Just pour your heart out." Friends cheered him up.

Arannya, who was a little tipsy, agreed to it and extended her left hand towards Gautam. They were sitting adjacent to each other, like always; even when Gautam was late, he'd smack the person sitting next to her and take that position.

Gautam kneeled and sought her permission to begin.

"Yes, yes, hero, go on," Arannya said as she sipped her wine.

"Arannya, a woman who is successful, independent, and dependable. A woman who outshines at her work every quarter and outdoes and pushes her own boundaries each year." Everyone went silent as if the spotlight was on these two.

"But I want to tell you how I look at her when I look at her. When I look at her, I look at the way she keeps tucking her deliberately loosened hair strands every now and then, I look at the way, at times, her true expressions of "What bullshit!" come on her face, and how nicely she steals her eyes from everyone around and takes another sip of her drink in an attempt to digest what her ears just heard. When I look at her, I look at the way she uses her hands as gestures while talking, how she talks while eating by hiding her mouth with her left hand, which makes me see her beautiful long fingers and withered-off nail polish from the corners still looking perfect.

When I look at her, I look at how she keeps rotating the ring she is wearing on the ring finger of her right hand. When I look at her, I see the way she crowns herself with her specs and keeps searching for them the next moment. I look at how she wants to curtain her dewy vulnerable eyes with those frames so that no one can ever deep dive in them and know how loving and emotional and vulnerable she is behind her strong woman stature. I look at the way she nibbles on her lips, gets cautious, and rushes to the washroom to apply some lipstick, for she has eaten it off her lips. When I look at her, I look at how uniquely beautiful she is, and when she smiles by making a frowning face and suddenly there's a bright smile, lastly I feel sad; I feel sad for the world because no one has been lucky enough till now to call her as their own."

There was complete silence. He was still holding her hand, and Arannya lifted her eyes and saw in his eyes for the first time; he shied away; she was seeing him in a different light. She felt the lump in her throat; no one ever described her so intricately.

She felt like hugging him. She was thinking about the abandoned lane again. And before she could take her hand off, the bell rang. It was the pizza delivery boy.

This was the night she felt maybe she was going too hard on her heart by not allowing anyone inside; should she just give it a chance? She looked into the mirror and told herself about how stupid and self-sabotaging that is and went off to sleep.

Love

Love unquestionably crowns the title of the most beautiful feeling in the world. It cannot be described in one sentence; it is a multidimensional emotion that drives the person's life. Love can be with a person, a thing, love for money, or for intangible things like God. No matter how hard one tries, they cannot deny its power. Love can move the mountains and destroy the whole world.

It doesn't care about age, religion, gender, or even species and opens up all the seven chakras in humans.

Love, however, is not limited to the number of times one can fall in it, but true love happens only once in a lifetime and more often than not at the wrong time.

Millions of poets and authors have written couplets and stories explaining the meaning of it, but no one could really put the feeling in just one sentence or story! Some say love is something that fights with all the hurdles and comes out winning; some say, What is love if not lost?; some say being able to live together is the greatest accomplishment of love; and some say true love sees its destination to its grave.

And then comes the institution of marriage, acting as a barometer for one's love towards the other. People are conditioned, or rather fooled, to agree that it is the final stage of love, but isn't love a thing to liberate the souls rather than something to be tied in a legalised bond with hundreds of acts?

The question here is: Is marriage really the destination of love? What if one finds love afterwards? Should it be just nipped in the bud? Or one must take courage and break free from all the societal and moral onus to be with 'the one'?

After all, you only live once!

Arannya was working for a renowned construction and consulting company, with architects, engineers, and even Vedic astrologers working together collaboratively. Her designs would get frequently rejected by the Feng Shui experts because of certain mis- arrangements in the placements of doors and windows. That used to make her go nuts, to make them understand the positioning of certain things at certain places is based on the structural load-bearing capacity and not from which direction the money would flow in.

It was Monday, and the director called for an urgent meeting of all the stakeholders of a project of which Arannya was a part. She reached just in time, but there were people who were still on the way, and the director despised latecomers. She sat in the second row of chairs encircling the first row, which was around the center table and was occupied by higher management. While she was busy checking her emails on the laptop, a man sat next to her panting, "Hi! Good morning", he said with a shaky voice. "Good morning," she replied, remaining in the same position and digging through her emails.

Sweetheart, time for breakfast,' her phone flashed with this notification. This was a food delivery app, the only thing that made her feel as if she was dating someone. Marketing strategies these days have turned more into emotional hinging than monetary benefits. The director started his monologue, and everyone encircling the round table had to pay attention, and people in the next row could steal a closed eye or two. One person who used to wear tinted thick glasses had the audacity to sleep right under the director's nose.

"Let's clap for the amazing work you guys did, and I hope you'll continue to do it." The room filled with clapping and broke the brave specky's nap.

It took almost an hour to finish the meeting; the director was happy with the work, and for this he has decided to treat everyone with wine and dine this coming Friday. The gathering Arannya despised.

Since she was connected to everyone just at the professional level, she didn't really have a confidant or friend in the office. Basically, she was a loner, a peaceful one, in fact. She couldn't ignore this as she had already been given feedback during the last performance meeting that she is impeccable when it comes to work, but she has to build rapport with her colleagues and also attend office luncheons or gatherings and other nonsensical things they did in the guise of team-building activities.

It's Friday already, and Arannya came home with a sullen face; she is in no mood to step out of the house. Lax was home as she had a late-night shoot. "What happened, Akka? Why do you look so grim?" She asked.

"I don't want to attend these stupid office parties," she babbled. Lax laughed. "I agree," she said, and asked if there was anything else Arannya was planning to do. She said she would sip wine, order pizza, and sleep.

"Stop being so boring, Akka. It'll be a crime if I don't force you to get ready and attend this party!" She said and ran towards her room to pick a dress for Arannya that she recently bought for herself. Arannya said it was too revealing for an official gathering and picked her black jumpsuit, which had brownish golden Swarovski stones around its tube neck.

Arannya got ready; while taking deep breaths, she spoke to herself, "I will go, have a glass of wine sitting at the counter, have some snacks, make myself visible in front of the director, manager, and any HR, and scoot off." "Whoosh," she breathed out at the count of 8 while practicing the 4-7-8 breathing technique that was prescribed to her by her psychologist to curb social anxiety.

"Akka, you're looking so pretty. Go put your feminine wiles to the test!" Lax wished her a good time.

She's heard that before; history has this subtle vice to repeat itself and sprinkle salt on the wounds of the past.

She arrived at the party wearing her black jumpsuit, paired with Lax's block heels. She kept her hair tied up in a high ponytail. It has been a year precisely since she attended such a party.

Everything happened as she pictured in her head. She searched for her manager and teammates first, greeted and complimented them, and reciprocated the compliments she received with an awkward smile. Then she saw her director, who was holding a glass of champagne, greet him and ask if he would like to have some snacks. He politely declined. There! She did the most difficult task of the day: to behave like a bootlicker, which she wasn't, but to just be there in the eyes of the director, she had to take this sour pill. She waved at some more people she knew from other departments, and one man from the group came walking towards her.

"Oh my God! You look gorgeous and smell edible!" Samar complimented her.

He was known to be a flirt in the office and had taken every single girl on a date, but her.

"Thank you," she replied and asked if he had seen Sharanya around. She was the HR she targeted to be noticed by. After this was done, she headed towards the bar section and ordered wine. One of her colleagues, Ridhima, came by and suggested that she order a margarita.

She ditched wine and decided to go by her suggestion; she never got to learn that the margaritas were spiked.

Sometimes a simple decision of choosing your drink can turn your life three hundred sixty degrees.

Arannya liked margaritas so much that even she didn't realise how many repeats she had had.

It was when she felt like puking she realised she reached her threshold. She went to the washroom and saw Ridhima puking; seeing that, she had an episode of contagious puking too.

She cleaned her mouth, did gargling, and got back in her senses. It's time for her to book the cab and leave the party.

She came out and went on the patio in search of getting a better network. There was a group of drunk people smoking cigarettes and cursing the director. Luckily the director by this time had left the party. She booked the cab and was eyeing the road. The patio was aesthetic, with the beautiful white garden chairs, and being on the middle floor of the building made it look like it was straight out of a Spanish home. She was taking a stroll, and a trail of wildly grown clover leaves caught her attention, leaving her exhilarated. She instantly recalled her memory with her Dadus story and how she used to keep on searching for a four-leaf clover for many years after he passed away. What if she finds the four-leaf clover here! She was examining each and every leaf very intricately. She was so lost in looking at them that she didn't notice there was a person observing her.

"Did you lose something?" asked the man.

"I'm looking for something I've never found!" A tipsy Arannya replied back this time too without noticing who the person was.

"Let me help you find it; my cab comes in 20." He said.

Arannya looked at him with amusement. He was the same man who sat next to her in that meeting. He introduced himself as Ray, and he said he knew her.

"Shit, where is my cab?" She checked her phone, and it was reaching her in 2 minutes.

"Hi, nice to meet you; gotta go. Bye, umm, Ray?" She took some time to recall his name again and asked a rhetorical question.

"Yeah, bye," he said. Arannya forgot to pick up her scarf that got untangled from her bag and fell on the ground.

Ray kept it to return it to her on Monday.

Ray's cab also came; he got in and shared the OTP. While on his way back, he was wondering what she must be searching for in the grass. He was noticing her throughout the party, right from how she adjusted her heel by kicking the feet on the ground as she entered the venue to her episodes with margaritas. But this wasn't the first time he noticed her, he used to subconsciously notice her even in the office, so discreet that even he himself never realised. There was something captivating in this lady; usually the female employees would always have their colleagues around them, and there she was all alone, still so complete in herself. Something was smelling so good in the cab. Ray looked at the scarf, and, making sure the driver was not noticing him, sniffed her scarf and literally got lost in the alluring fragrance. He did it three more times, and the third time the driver caught him doing that and looked at him as if he were some perv. Embarrassed, Ray stuffed the black and beige geometric print silk scarf in his pockets. Ray got mesmerised with the smell; that night he slept by spreading it over his face.

The next morning he woke up with a hangover from the cocktail that he had; he noticed the scarf and felt a bit disgusted about himself for behaving like a paedophile, clinging on to a little girl's belongings. He creeped out and kept the scarf in the cupboard.

Ray, a man in his early forties, questioning every decision he has made in his life, going through midlife crises like every other man his age, has a wife and a son and a pretty enviable, successful life. He was the owner of quite an attractive personality; given his age, he by default fell into the category of one of those men in the office who were rarely noticed since they were already taken. He has had a close group of colleagues, his teammates, who he used to hang around with; if going on lunch together can be counted in. He was the Senior manager for the Safety and QC department. He was that handsome introvert who everyone wanted to know more about. People hardly saw him talking loudly or laughing.

But if one were to notice him properly, they would know that he must have been quite a catch in his early ages. Nobody can tell he's in his forties. He has maintained himself well. Clear skin, a wheatish skin tone, always clean-shaven, wearing an ironed shirt without tucking it in and ironed jeans with Jordans made him look young for his age. Having an alluring persona with a height of 6'2, he could easily make women go weak on their knees.

It was one of the Mondays after a few weeks from the party that Arannya and Ray bumped into each other in the parking lot. Ray gestured a 'hey' by moving his eyebrows up, and Arannya smiled back.

Arannya wondered if she had met Ray in person before. But she couldn't recollect. And Ray wondered how weird it was of him to do that; it was just acting out of his character. Both of them drove their way back home.

While waiting at the signal, Arannya couldn't stop thinking hard about whether she ever had a conversation with him, and Ray was thinking if she remembers that they had a conversation.

It was quite unusual for both of them to be occupied with each other's thoughts. It was best to divert their minds off each other, they thought, and get engrossed in their mundane lives.

But their Cupid just woke up from a long sleep and had a long list of tasks to take care of. He must still be hungover from the hibernation that he lost his sense of judgement while he shot his arrow towards these two.

Ridiculously, "*Love*" never got schooled about right or wrong and who it has to bud with. Age, gender, relation, race, and ethnicity—nothing matters; it surpasses and challenges the age-old traditions and folklores of humankind, and hence it is not everyone's cup of tea; only a few who dared to pick the cup realised it's not filled with tea but elixir.

Till now both of them had their worldly conditioned understanding of love, but they didn't know they were among the chosen few who were going to experience this ecstasy in its purest form. And the colour of this love wasn't red as the human claims; the colour of love is "white," which is going to wash off all the other colours in life, and only the divinity of this true feeling would have a space to dwell.

This happened on a Wednesday when, during the lunch hour, the canteen was unusually bustling.

Arannya, tied up with some work, arrived late only to find no space for her to sit; moreover, her usual place, where there was a high chair and she could face the outside view of coconut trees and eat peacefully, was occupied too.

She brought the lunch and tried her luck to find a place or at least someone who would finish up and vacate the seat, but that wasn't her day, it seemed. She got awkward and was ruminating on her loner persona. It wasn't a very difficult task to walk up to someone and ask if she could sit, but that just wasn't her. Finally, someone called her. "Arannya! Arannya, come over here; we have a place here." It was Sujith; he was working in the QC department, and he was the first person she spoke with on her first day in the office.

She went and was thankful for him being considerate about her plight.

"Thanks, Sujith! What happened to people today? Everyone broke at the same time for lunch or what?"

Aarnaya said as she adjusted her seat and pulled it closer to the table.

"You bet! There's something wrong with people today," said Sujith as he stuffed his mouth with the halwa.

Arannya was like a horse, so focused in only one direction that she didn't realise she was sitting right next to Ray.

It was only when Ray finished his lunch and got up that they saw each other. They exchanged a warm smile. Suddenly she felt butterflies in her stomach; he was no exception.

"That's something!" commented Sujith.

"What?!" She was baffled as if he saw through her heart.

"Ray 'NEVER' really smiles!" He passed the statement and got up from the table too.

Her lunch was almost done, and she noticed the whiff of fragrance that came as Ray passed by, reminding her about the brief encounter she had with him at the party. She clenched her left fist and hit not so softly on her forehead.

Now, they say when the Cupid in your life is stubborn about making things happen, he will make every possible or impossible encounter with that person. Arannya and Ray started to bump into each other more often than usual; it was purely unintentional, but somehow they had moments where she went to take coffee and he also went at the same time, and when she turned, she saw him and couldn't control her blushing. Like they were arriving and leaving almost at the same time and ended up parking their cars next to each other.

One day Arannya was wearing a saree in the office, which was a sight to behold for the entire male community. She was wearing a light pink silk saree with a sky blue border. During the lunch break she went deliberately late so that she could sit with Ray and his team, and she didn't even understand why she had that thought. Something definitely changed in her.

She sat with Sujith and asked him in the most casual way about where Ray is. Sujith was like a sniffer dog, and he asked, "Why do you ask, Haan!?" With a sarcastic tone and a very bad smile. She shook his reaction off.

Arannya was eagerly waiting for Ray to come and see her because she knew she looked great that day and had received a lot of compliments. But for some reason even she couldn't fathom this urge to have Ray see her and compliment her.

And then he arrived, wearing a dreamy light pink T-shirt that made him look instantly 10 years younger. To her disappointment, Ray acted neutral and just gestured with the left eyebrow raised and a generic smile.

They were sitting opposite each other, and Sujith, out of his habit, teased Arannya and whispered in her ear, "Same colour! Not bad! Not bad!" Arannya gave him an insouciant shrug. This time she was confused if her expressions or enquiries about Ray had been suspectful, or if it was just that Sujith had mystical intuitive powers.

Sujith finished his lunch and left. It was just Ray and Arannya now; neither of them spoke to each other. But they somewhere knew that there were some undefined vibrations flowing through them, and they were liking it too as their speed of eating the food decreased substantially. They had a couple of eye contacts, mostly stolen and veiled ones, but it was evident that they both were noticing each other.

Nevertheless, killing Arannya's expectation, Ray did not say anything to her. And she smiled at herself, thinking if she is really that stupid. There was no way a man who is the manager would compliment her out in the open, or maybe it didn't mean anything to him at all; fair enough! She consoled her heart and tried to be happy with the tonnes of compliments she received from almost everyone. The most creepy was from Samar, who told her she looked like a *Candy Floss* and how he used to gulp the whole thing at once while he was a child.

Arannya took a cab to work since she wasn't comfortable driving in a saree. On top of that, she was super late. It was Lax's turn to pick her up from the office as she took her car.

"Lax, where are you? If it's going to take time, then I will take the cab." She said on the call.

"We'll be there in 5 Akka!" Lax replied.

In the next five minutes she was there, but someone else was driving the car; it was Gautam. Arannya didn't pay attention when Lax said, "We'll be there.".

"Hi... Haaaaaaaay!" The good ol' dramatic Gautam sighed at the scenery in front of him as he saw Arannya for the first time in a saree. Arannya blushed and pulled the rear door.

"Wait! Stop." He exclaimed.

"Do you want me to be a sinner? Let me have the pleasure of opening the door for you, my lady." Saying that, he got down from the car.

"And you, kindly F off to the backseat." He commanded Lax, and she obliged like a sincere servant. "Yes, sir," Lax mocked him.

"Cut the drama, you too!" Arannya said and sat on the front seat; however, she wanted to hide; she was enjoying all the attention she was receiving.

"Lax, you were saying you had to visit someone, right? Should I drop you first, and then I will drop your Akka?" Gautam asked.

"No, I will visit him overmorrow." Lax replied and continued to scroll through her phone. Suddenly she realised what he was indicating and said, "Oh! Yes, you're right! At times you surprise me with your brain, Goo!"

"Akka, I need to visit someone..."

"Yes, I know you guys! No need for this drama; let's go home now." Arannya cut her short.

As they reached their building, Lax got down near the lobby to collect her parcel. Arannya and Gautam went to the basement to park the car. Gautam was indeed a happy-go-lucky person, and Arannya couldn't deny that he was an absolute gentleman. As she was about to open the door, he stopped her. Got down and opened the door for her.

"You are mad!" she said as she blushed.

"Can I say, 'For you', or would that be too cheesy?" Gautam winked.

"Shall we?" Arannya signalled towards the lift.

They were staying on the 17th floor, and there was no one in the lift.

Arannya could sense Gautam wanted to say something, and not proving her wrong, he broke the silence: "Will there ever be a day when you will consider my feelings towards you?" Gautam asked earnestly. This was not his trait.

Cling! The lift opened.

Arannya thanked the timing. She got anxious with the thought of being really happy in the future, but she has already experienced what happiness brings along with it: 'destruction!'

It was only in the future, during her pre-marriage counselling, that she got to learn that she was dealing with cherophobia.

Arannya thought that she was a strong individual and free person, not caged and on her own, but she didn't realise that by closing herself off to the world, she had built an invisible cage around herself; wherever she goes, she is still caged. Only the powerful force of true love could break her free; she just had to put some faith in the unknown and step out; unbeknownst to her, love was just round the corner. This was her liberation. Something she had never imagined in her wildest dreams.

It was the beginning of autumn already, the season Arannya loved the most since she used to take solo trips during this time to meet her true self, where she would let her guard down and feel what she wanted to feel, crying as much for her loveless life.

The cold breeze during the day when the sun is still shining bright gave her the best of feelings. Chilly mornings and moist evenings brought lots of nostalgia from her past life. But when the divinely beautiful evening marries the mysterious night sky, it pinches her heart, and the air gets filled in the lonely corner of the red room. When the memories of her failed relationships return, she mechanises them in a constructive way and believes they played a vital role in making her what she is today. Rather than focusing on the pain, she reminisces about the euphoria she experienced.

The most hurtful thing for her was she never really got a proper closure to any of them; one relationship left her guessing, one suddenly ceased to exist, and another just ended out of the blue! Whenever she thinks of Karan's apathetic behaviour towards the catastrophe, it hurts her and makes her heart bleed. Even if she never wanted to go back to him, since he was already betrothed, she somewhere still hoped that he'd break free from his onus and come to her. Alas! Such things happen only in movies and romantic novels. But surprisingly, in between all this, she could sense a mysterious pull towards one person; she had one name running in her mind all the time: Ray!

She hated the concept of infidelity, and being the 'third person' in anyone's relationship was no less than a grave sin in her world. People often reason it with bizarre circumstances, but in the end, what is wrong is wrong. Despite how virtuous Arannya was, her "I'd never be the third person in anyone's life" principle had her fall flat on the ground.

'Never say never,' they say!

After Ray's display of cool-as-a-cucumber behaviour towards her, the thought of somehow making a place in his inner circle became a far-fetched ambition for Arannya. She tried her best to keep an indifferent approach towards anything related to Ray. She tried to finish her lunch before the cafeteria got crowded and get back to her work to avoid any expected encounter with him. To avoid her heart's forbidden desires, she started to reciprocate Gautam's efforts in an attempt to stop thinking about Ray, but she failed because some invisible force was pulling her towards him more and more each passing day! The limerence filled her with guilt. Obsessing over someone who is a decade older than her, having a happy married life, made her hate herself, but her heart felt like a separate entity to her; it wasn't in her control. With an attempt to stop such illicit thoughts, she decided to divert her heart and mind towards Gautam.

Gautam often used to sing her the Hosanna song whose lyrics meant, *"If he has two hearts, he will give her the second heart too, even though she's already broken the first one."* Arannya knew Gautam was an easygoing guy and would take things lightly, so she found her refuge in him.

It was a Friday, and Arannya was missing Ray terribly; she thought maybe she shouldn't have distanced herself completely and at least kept joining him for lunch. She craved to just have a glimpse of him and reasoned her fancy with, 'That's not a crime in any book!' Hence she decided to go for lunch a little late and join their table again.

"Oh! Look who's back!" Sujith said to Pavan as he waved Arannya and signalled her to join them at the table. Arannya waved back, took her food, and sat next to a vacant chair, with a hope Ray would turn up. To her disappointment, he did not, and she couldn't gather the courage to ask about him. She finished her lunch, and while walking towards the washing area to keep the plates, Sujith came near her and whispered, "He went on site today," as if he read her mind. If Cupid had a face, it was Sujith's in Arannya's life.

'Had lunch, Master?' This was Gautam's text. She saw but didn't respond.

Arannya was no different when it came to the law of attraction towards the opposite gender. She chose to ignore the one who was ready to give her the world and got pulled towards the one who is not reciprocating and acknowledging her 'unspoken' feelings. When love takes charge, logic sees the exit door, Arannya completely ignores the fact that Ray is unbeknownst to what's in her heart, and criticizes him for not knowing something she never expressed! Women aren't that complicated, are they?

This whim of running towards something that is impossible to achieve has destroyed many hearts and even lives. By the time she realised this, she was already low-key obsessed with him.

Arannya's past experiences have damaged her ways beyond her imagination. And her ignorant approach towards those hurt never allowed her to heal. She believed that anything normal isn't meant for her, and she will always get happiness the hard way. Hence, when Gautam approached her, she never took it seriously. Her philophobia kept him at bay. While in Ray's case, she knew there was no destination to it since he already belonged to someone else. She knew it's only going to hurt her in the end. This gave her a sense of strange satisfaction that she knew what the result was going to be and thus could keep her emotions in control. But she was a fool not to know that love doesn't have a reputation to dwell in a controlled environment. She decided to love him, knowing that she'd never have him, ergo no heartbreak! In her past she intended to bring her relationships to their goal but was always at the receiving end; this time she'd walk from the grave towards life, like trying to breathe life into an inanimate object.

It was like playing a losing game. This time she deliberately put her heart on bait.

After work that day she was feeling blue and just wanted to have a few pints in solace. She went to her usual place, 'Soft Jazz Cafe,' but there were people that knew her since she was a regular, so she decided to go to a place where no one knows her and she can have her space. She took the car off parking and went to 'Ferrum Mount,' which was on the way towards her home.

She gave the car keys to the valet and went inside. This is such a nice place, she said in her mind. There were sections, like one near the pond that was the quietest and one near the dance floor that was the loudest, but sitting by the pond meant being a feast for the mosquitoes; hence she headed towards her preferred spot, the bar counter. Easier to communicate with the bartender, plus she usually gets a couple of complimentary drinks too; if not that, her 60 would be poured as 90.

If the love failures are overlooked, she was certainly lucky otherwise.

"Hi Ma'am, welcome. What would you like to have?" Asked the barman, donning a pleasant warm smile.

"Umm, I would like to have..."

"Anything but Margarita!" She got interrupted by someone; she turned to find and couldn't believe her eyes! Is that really HIM! Her eyes got stuck with his, and she couldn't take them off for a nice long 6 seconds.

Both of them experience the feeling of kama muta.

"Hello!" Ray snapped his fingers at an astonished Arannya.

"Hi!" This time she behaved like Gautam, lovestruck.

"Hi!" he said and asked if he could sit next to her. While in fact he was already on the next chair, which she occupied.

"Don't embarrass me; I guess you were sitting here already. I should be the one asking this question," she chuckled.

"Excuse me, ma'am, what can I make for you?" asked the barman.

"Oh! Yes, what are you having?" she asked Ray.

"Scotch," he said, "Ballantine."

"What's your poison?" he asked.

"Whisky! JD," she answered, her eyes were dilating.

"Shall I make it a 60, ma'am?" The guy asked in a voice enough to distract from her amusement, and she nodded.

They both raised the glass and cheered.

"So, Arannya! Tell me. How's everything going?"

"Things are going as usual; the BAK project is off the books, and the director will hold another round of meetings for its post mortem." She answered.

"And?" asked Ray as he sipped his drink.

"And, we will be having our office renovated soon, and I am on the planning team." She answered again.

"And?" This time Ray directly looked into her eyes while he sipped the remaining whiskyfrom his glass. She could see he was smiling.

"And the weather is nice today." She started to get nervous. She sensed that Ray is already down a few pegs. Each time he asked, "And?" he maintained a very rigid eyegaze. As if he was deciphering her through his eyes.

"And nothing, you say!" She acted cool and sipped her drink.

"Hmmm," Ray said with the most charming smile, and this was the time she saw he was the owner of two adorable and perfect dimples! Which was adding four stars to his beauty. He was beautiful! Handsome is too non-effective an adjective to describe him. If a person is meeting him for the first time, they would have second thoughts if he is married yet.

"Repeat, please," Ray asked the barman.

Ray took Arannya's glass and said, "This too."

"Arannya! such a unique name. Be ready to tell me the meaning of it and check what you want to eat. I will be back in a jiffy." Having said that, he double-tapped on her head as if she was some child, and he went to the loo.

Arannya lost her heart this time, as if it broke free from the cage she created around her. Like a prisoner who was innocent and convicted falsely, it eloped from there at the first chance to escape. Arannya was in a trance. She still couldn't believe if this was really happening or if it was one of the sessions where her subconscious was orchestrating the dream for her.

They spoke about different topics, like politics, weather, the future of the company, how the city is getting overcrowded, etc.; she couldn't recall most of the conversations. But when the conversation took a personal turn, this is where she felt she could let go of her mask, which she wears for the world, and be her authentic self.

"Tell me something: Why don't you have any friends in the office?" Asked Ray.

"I like to keep my personal and professional life separate," she said dramatically.

"No, really, I have seen you moving around alone. Doesn't anyone fit your standards?"

"No, not like that. This is just the way I am. I don't want to connect people outside the work boundaries; this way I keep myself from getting hurt in any way."

"And what about happiness? Don't you want to be happy and have fun?"

"Been there, done that!" She asserted.

"What about your love life?" He asked.

"HaHaHa!" She laughed devilishly. By this time, Arannya was 4 pegs down and Ray 3 more over that.

"Now you have asked the correct question! Actually, you know, I am convinced that I am jinxed in the matters of love; I must have done something terrible in my past life that my love life is fucked up! Every time I gave it a chance, I failed, and each time more severely, more pathetically. All I ever wanted was one person who I love to love me back, but it never happened as if I am cursed. I mean, what have I done so wrong to never have one person who loves me just for me, takes efforts for me, and gets butterflies as he sees me? Why? Am I not good-looking? Am I not doing great in my life? Then why am I ever so struggling in this area of my life? Is this too much to ask for?" Said she in one breath, as if she recited this monologue only for times like this.

"Yes!" Answered Ray as he bit the fish fingers.

"What? Are you for real?" Arannya checked her glass was empty and asked the barman to refill it.

"Yes, that is too much to ask for!" Ray repeated himself. "What you are asking for is everything! And nobody ever gets everything!" He concluded.

"Elaborate, Please!" Arannya knew that she got the hit now as her vision started to blur. She spoke to herself in her mind that she is okay; she is not that drunk. To keep a check on her senses, she asked herself what her name was, what her employee ID was, and answering that correctly means she is still good.

"See, you are doing great in your career, have a well-to-do family, possess good health, and have money in your bank; there's one area of your life that upsets you: love. If you receive even that, then what will you chase in your life? What will be your Ikigai?" He said, and gestured to the barman to get the check by enacting signing in the air.

"Wooo Wooo Wooo! Someone lost their senses here!" Arannya leans on the table, giving support to her oscillating body.

"Everyone around me seems to be doing great in every sector of their life; it's just me because I am jinxed!" she stated firmly.

"Take a closer look, Arannya. I am sure you will find the answer." He said as he gave her his hand to get down from the chair.

Since both of them were drunk, Ray booked a cab and asked her about her address; she mumbled something, but he couldn't understand. He took her ID card, which was dangling out of her handbag, and told the address to the driver.

They came out, and he opened the door for her and made sure she sat properly. He sat in the front, and while he was sharing the OTP, the valet came running towards him and handed him her car keys. Arannya had already dozed off, so he kept the keys in his pocket. Ray told him he will pick the car tomorrow and tipped the valet.

In about 10 minutes they reached near her building. He opened the door for her and shook her by her shoulder. "Hey, get up; you are home."

"Hmmm." Arannya's eyes were red; she was totally knocked out, but even in this state she could see Ray's beautiful face and the dimples outshining it.

"Yeah! Oh my God, I'm so sorry for the trouble." She was apologetic.

"Hey! You don't have to," he said.

She came out and closed the door. Still leaning against it, Ray felt she wouldn't be able to make it on her own, so he requested the driver to wait for 5 minutes till he escorted her to her place. He asked her the floor; she said 17th. In an attempt to keep her from falling, he held her by her shoulders, his right hand on her right shoulder and his left hand holding her by her left arm. The lift opened, and Arannya, even though she was drunk, was aware of what was happening. She was in fact tripping more on the guilty pleasure. She thought this is the best time to say anything she can and later blame it on the alcohol!

The elevator reached her floor, and as she stepped out, she turned towards him and said, "I have one complaint against you!"

Ray's intoxication just flushed down as soon as he heard that. His eyes became wide out of curiosity, and he stopped the closing elevator doors with his hands.

He was just eager for her to say more.

"That day..." She started and pressed her lips inward; she was hesitating.

"Go on, I am all ears," Ray said, flashing his dimples.

"That day when I wore a saree, everyone in the office complimented me, but you. I was very disheartened," she frowned.

In her response, Ray smiled and sought apologies. She smiled back and started to leave when she heard him call her name, "Arannya!" She stopped and looked back. "That day, you were looking like magic; the silver bangles were complimenting your attire perfectly, though it was evident you had a little difficulty in walking wearing a saree. Next time try wearing flats rather than heels, and if you would wear those bindis that are shaped like a droplet of water instead of the round one, it will just be perfect. Good night," he waved, and the door closed.

"Good...night." This was definitely a dream! She couldn't take more miracles for the day, went straight, and crashed.

The next day in the morning, around 11 am, she woke up with an obvious hangover; a heavy head and dizziness made it difficult for her to get up from the bed. With half-closed eyes, she tried to reach her phone, which had fallen under the bed. She tried harder, but her hands couldn't reach her phone. Irked, she got up, and suddenly all the things that happened last night flashed in her mind! She held her head with both her hands and jumped out of embarrassment, "No, no, no, no, no, no, no."

"Noooo, noooo, that was a dream. That was a dream." She was walking briskly in her room like a pendulum.

Lax, who was also half asleep, came to her room to see if everything was okay.

"Akka! What happened? Are you ok?"

"Laaaaaaaax..." "I am doomed," she said, thrusting on the floor.

She told her everything she could remember and was surprised over the fact that Lax is so cool about everything. "Ohhhh! That's so romantic!" said Lax.

"Are you crazy! I am so embarrassed to even face him now."

"Chill, Akka, from where I am seeing, this has the potential to bud into a very hot and torrid affair!" Lax sounds cheesy.

"Stop it, Lax. Anyway, I will seek his apologies and make sure this doesn't happen ever again. Like *never ever!*" Arannya breathes out.

Her phone vibrated; it was a call from an unknown number. She rejected the call.

It rang again; this time she turned it to silent and asked Lax to check on RealCaller: Whose number was that? Arannya hardly received calls from unknown numbers. What if the caller is one of her relatives asking her, "When are you getting married?"

"It's Narayan," Lax said.

"Narayan! Who could that be?" Arannya wondered.

The phone rang again; this time she answered the call.

"Yes!"

"Hey, good morning! This is Ray." said the person on the other side.

"Huh," she was dumbstruck.

"Hi!" she trembled.

"I got your car; can you come down to collect the keys? Or should I hand it over to the guard?"

"Sheesh! I completely forgot about my car. Where are you? Wait, I am coming." Having said that, Arannya got up, looked at herself in the mirror, brushed her hair a few strokes, applied lip gloss, and sprinkled some perfume.

Lax, who was observing this, was overwhelmed because she had never seen Arannya this excited about anything ever, even when she received the Best Employee award!

Arannya, failing to hide her excitement, asked Lax, "How am I looking?"

"Like a teenager going on their first date! Hahaha! *'Never ever,'* it seems." She laughed, and Arannya hugged her, which again was not her body language.

She reached the ground floor and saw Ray had parked her car in the visitors lane and was waiting for her, standing near the car.

Oh! What a morning, she sighed, as if her good karma finally started to pay off. As she walked towards him with butterflies in her stomach, she saw he was immersed in his phone, wearing a blue Polo T-shirt over beige 3/4ths with Crocs, and the aviators succeeded in making him look like Arannya's batchmate. Was that Ray's motive? Only Ray had an answer to that.

"Hi! I am so sorry for all the trouble," she apologised.

"That's alright! You don't have to be sorry for everything. Just live it up at times." He said and removed his sunglasses.

"Here." He handed over the keys to her.

"Can I drop you?" she asked.

"You can, but then again I'd ask the same, and we'll be just stuck in an unbreakable loop!" He laughed.

"Hahaha, Yup, so how will you go back now? Cab?" she asked.

"I thought so, but the metro is just 100 m away from here, and it's been ages since I travelled in it, so that's my adventure for this weekend." He replied.

"Okay, have a happy weekend." She said,

"You too." He replied.

And they went their own ways.

"That's it?!" Lax was disappointed; she thought Arannya would ask him to come up or at least make some plans with him. But none of that happened.

"Yeah! And that's all it will be in this case! So please don't have any high hopes with this one, Lax. It's fun to think about it, but in reality it is like burning yourself in hell. So hold your horses." Arannya requested. She was saying this to Lax, but in reality, she was warning herself about the metaphysical ramifications.

"Yeah, fine, if that's that, then let me call Goo and check if that dumbo is planning anything for the weekend or not." Lax unlocked her phone to make him a call.

"Oh! Please, kiddo, spare me for the day!" Arannya begged and went back to sleep.

Saturday went in getting rid of the hangover and ruminating about last night for her,

And Sunday went on deciding what clothes she was going to wear to the office on Monday. Will they be talking about what happened Friday night? Should she just text him asking if he can meet her in the evening? Even after knowing that this wasn't right, she couldn't stop thinking about him. She did not feel that this was wrong even once; was her sense of judgement on vacation, or had she just become nonchalant towards the moral compass of her life? Whatever it was, she was feeling alive after a long time. And she did not want to let go of this feeling.

She was happy.

On the other hand, Ray believed this was all just normal and it meant nothing more than an act of camaraderie. He knew if he dug deeper into these emotions, something uncommon would come up; hence he decided not to pay any heed to thinking deeper in this regard and just go with the flow.

One thing was common: both of them thought it was one-sided.

Then came Monday. Arannya arrived in the office just in time. She wore a muted yellow Chickenkari kurti with the water droplet-shaped maroon bindi, which she bought the previous day. She wore her exclusive perfume and tied her favourite watch. She felt good about how she was looking that day. Someone from her team even called her, "Hey, Sunflower!" giving a shot to her already blooming confidence. This was just the start of the day.

She hung in there patiently until the lunch break. Time was ticking slowly, and her excitement to see him was making her anxious. She set an alarm for 2 hours and finished all the important tasks for the day. It was about time. Her heart raced, and she started to sweat. She took her compact powder and lipstick and went to the restroom for a touch-up.

She looked in the mirror and fixed her bindi and blushed. A girl came out of the washroom and passed her a very condescending look. Arannya pretended to ignore and went straight to the cafeteria.

She took her lunch and went to Sujith, who signalled her already. There was a seat vacant next to Ray and one next to Sujith. She went on to sit next to Sujith, but he asked her to sit on the other chair since Samar was joining them. Samar was from Arannya's team, and this was one of his many efforts to hit on her.

"Hey!" She greeted Ray, who was focused on his food.

"Hi!" He responded without turning towards her and continued eating.

The entire lunch Aranaya got stuck with Samars balderdash.

Sujith finished his lunch and got up; he even asked Samar to come along, but he was insistent on sitting until she finished her lunch. She somehow responded to all his questions through gritted teeth and gasps, but Samar kept on going.

Ray also finished and got up; she felt weird, but what could she do after all? Who is she to even complain? Even today he did not see her Bindi, or he did? There was a tectonic push and pull building between them.

Later that day, saddened by his ignorance, she finished all her tasks and went home early.

She opened the wine bottle that she bought on her way back home along with some ingredients to prepare her signature lasagna. She turned the music on, poured herself a glass of wine, and started to prepare her dinner. Cooking has been a proven therapy for a long and tiring day for her, and as she chopped the veggies, she vented out her outburst.

'What is wrong with you?' She asked herself aloud since Laxmi wasn't home.

'What are you thinking? Have you lost your mind? You need to stop!' She warned herself and hit her head with the wooden spatula.

'Ouch!' That was a hard hit.

'Focus on your things, your career; you need to move out of the country and see the world. If everything seems so overwhelming, at least give a chance to Gautam! He deserves it in every manner. You idiot!' She concluded her self-talk.

'*Ting*' Her phone chimed. It was Ray's message.

She wanted to throw the phone away and just block him.

But what if it's related to work or if he is in some trouble? After all these years her pessimistic thought process never left her.

She unlocked her phone and read the text, "Why did you leave early today? All Ok? And yes, that's exactly the type of Bindi that I mentioned the other day. Did justice!"

Finished! Defeated! All the angst vanished in a snap! She nibbled her thumbnail and laughed at her miserable state.

For the heart wants what it wants!

Ray somewhere knew maybe he was the reason she must have left early, but sending her that message wasn't a very good idea, he thought after he pressed the send button.

This is definitely going to give her a different impression. But he was just playing along without knowing this is going to bring them a lot of joy followed by even larger griefs. Come to think of it, even Ray started to behave like a teenager.

The next three days Ray was on leave as his health was not well. Arannya tried hard to stop her urge from calling him. What if his wife picks up the call? What if she is around and she asks who she is? To be a trouble to him in any manner was the last thing on her mind. So she texted him on the office messenger.

"Hi, I just wanted to check if you are good and will be able to join the meeting that is scheduled for tomorrow." There was no meeting; she just framed the message in such a manner that even if his wife happened to see it, she wouldn't be suspicious.

Ray saw the message and smiled; he understood what she did there.

He replied to her saying he is getting better and will try to join the meeting tomorrow.

It was a relief for her.

But even the next day and the day after, he did not return to the office, and Arannya thought it's better to leave him be and practice patience. However, her courage got a little boost, and she asked Sujith about his whereabouts.

It was Friday, and even though he wasn't fully recovered, he showed up in the office wearing a mask. Arannya, on the other hand, was slogging through the day. Ray was waiting for the lunch break so that he'd get to meet her and surprise her. She didn't go to the office cafeteria for lunch because what's the point, she thought, and ordered her lunch at her desk.

He was sad, and so was she. At times a simple act of communication can save you from melancholy.

While going back home, she was surprised to find his car in the parking lot, which means he came, and he did not inform her! So, she took her phone out to make a call. But then she stopped and analysed; if he wanted to meet her or see her, he'd have done that. By making him a call, she will make herself look like a fool and come out as clingy, needy, and whatnot. Moreover, he is in no way under any obligation to inform her; the whole situation was a bummer for her.

Should I wait in the car for him? She thought. And she stayed back in her car, without turning it on, to avoid being seen by others. Which made her sweat like a pig.

It's been an hour and he still hasn't shown up. Others came and went by, and she triumphed in dodging their attention.

Finally he came and ran his eyes to see her. As soon as she saw him, she turned on the ignition, acted as if she didn't see him, and dashed out of the parking lot.

Why did she do that? When she was waiting for him? Even she couldn't make sense of it. Ray maintained his neutral demeanour.

'What did I just do?' 'Haven't I made it obvious?' 'Did he see me? Oh hell, of course he knows my car.' 'Why do I put myself in such a spot?' 'I'm a fool, period.' She reprimanded herself.

She reached her place and vacillated between calling or not calling him. Clenching and unclenching her fists, she took a deep breath and calmed herself down. Turned the music loud in her headphones and swayed on the balcony swing.

Ray thought it was better to let this slide and focus on his mundane life.

The next week in the office was like hide and seek. On Monday she went for lunch, and he did not join for lunch, thinking he may have overwhelmed her; on Tuesday she didn't join, thinking she had made things awkward for him, and on Wednesday both had their team lunches. On Wednesday, when she went to get coffee, he was there talking to her manager. He said hi; she got tongue-tied, and as much as she wanted to respond, she ended up with a creepy smile with all her teeth visible; she abused her manager in her mind and went away. That day she again stayed low in her car for him to come and act as if she was on her way. They finally bumped into each other. He wanted to talk to her, but another guy from his team was with him. She started the car; they exchanged glances from a distance, and she left, another failed attempt at having a conversation.

What an arsehole week this was! She cried over her fate.

The next day, Thursday, she decided that come what may, she would go have lunch with him and his team and ask him if he could stay back to have a word with her. That day, the entire office was summoned in the cafeteria to collect doughnuts since they won some award.

After lunch, Arannya mustered the courage to walk up to him while he was taking the fennel seeds from the counter.

"Can you pour me some?" she asked.

"Yeah, you need the sugar-coated one?"

"Just the roasted ones, thanks."

There was a hullabaloo in the cafeteria at the place of doughnut distribution. Some people from the higher management were blabbering about how they achieved success in this difficult quarter and won the award.

"Do you have a moment?" she asked finally.

"Yes, tell me?"

"Can we have Narayan here, please?" somebody called him.

"Ray I mean Ray! Can we have you here, please? Let's hear from the horse's mouth, everyone." And everyone started to clap and look at him.

He was startled and went to them.

'Narayan' was his actual name, but since the time he joined the industry, he was most popularly known as Ray, a nickname given to him by his first boss, and it became his alias ever since.

In the evening after work, even after so many unsuccessful attempts to have a conversation with him, she didn't give up and stayed back in her car again. He came to the parking lot, and somewhere he knew she would be there waiting for him. As she was about to step out of the car, Gargi from his team came out of nowhere and asked if he could drop her at the nearest metro; for the gentleman he was known to be, there was no way he'd have refused to help her.

She saw him; he saw her. They were literally dying inside to just talk to each other, but circumstances were not in their favour.

She stomped her legs back in the car and closed the door, buckled herself, and drove off. She saw in the rearview mirror that he was holding his car door and watching her leave.

Today she wasn't angry; she was just sad, and somewhere she knew even he was looking forward to having a word with her. She just knew it. So much so she could bet her life on it.

The next day, with a new will and determination, she got ready for work, wore a white colour Kurti, and the same Bindi of 'water droplet shape.' Smelt like an absolute piece of dessert and hit the office.

During lunch time, Sujith praised her that she is smelling so good.

"That's a very personal remark!" Ray said abruptly.

Sujith got a little awkward, but he took it with a pinch of salt; Ray was his boss after all.

Arannya couldn't make sense of what just happened; this was the first time he said something that was directly related to her.

"So, Miss. Arannya, it's Friday! What time are you leaving?" Ray asked.

Sujith acted deaf after the fresh escapade.

She was convinced that Ray was on some substance.

"By 7," she replied.

"Okay," he said and got up from the table.

As soon as he left, both Sujith and Arannya exchanged puzzled glances.

It was 6:30 PM, and she wrapped her work before 5 itself. She cleared off all the last-minute hiccups and went to the parking lot exactly around 7, with a hope to meet him.

To her disappointment, his car wasn't there; he left already. He left! It was 6:50 PM, and she literally felt pity for herself; she apologised to her innocent heart for putting itself through such situations.

'It's whisky time, baby!' She cheered herself up and turned the music in her car loud with the song and sang, "*It's just me, myself, and I, a solo ride until I die, 'cause I have me for life.*"

Her eyes were closed when she was singing this, and as she opened her eyes, she saw Ray standing beside her car and enjoying her little concert. "Oh! Oh my God!!" She turned off the music and rolled her glass down.

"Friday started early for someone today!" He laughed.

"I thought you left!"

"That's why you seemed so happy!?"

"Stop pulling my leg," she frowned.

"I was asking if you can drop me at my friend's place; he stays near your place." he asked

"Oh! Of course I can." She was rather delighted.

"May I?" He asked if he could sit.

"Sure, yeah,"

"The thing is, my car broke down, so I took a cab today," he said as he sat and closed the door.

"Okay." She tried not to turn towards him and show her face that turned pink.

But she was blushing so hard that it was impossible for him not to notice.

"All good?" He asked.

"Yeah! Perfect," she said, and the Hawayein song started to play on the radio.

What could be more perfect than this? But there was more.

They drove past 'Ferrum Mount,' and he said, "By the way, I am in no rush to reach my friend; if you have some time, we can have a pint and eat something."

As if he had the key to her heart and saw what's in it. She didn't say a word and took the next U-turn.

"Same place?" He asked where she wanted to sit.

"No, Graden this time," she replied.

The ambience was spectacular and serene. Fairy lights thrown asymmetrically on the naturally grown trees and bushes, garden chairs carved out of wooden logs, and wooden tables made it all look picture perfect. They picked the middle table.

Something was undeniably happening between them, but that something was that something that was missing from their lives; therefore, they chose not to brood about this.

Were they doing anything wrong? No! Were they doing something right? No! But whatever it was, they were attracted towards each other, and this they were going to realise tonight.

"This ginger beer is really nice!" She said as she gulped.

"Try white beer too!" He sipped and passed the glass to her.

"Oh! Sorry, I will ask for a spare glass," he said.

Before he could call someone, she sipped from his glass.

"Hmmm. Really worth it." She liked the taste.

"You can try mine too," she said.

And they ended up sipping each other's beer in turn.

"So, tell me something about your family?" asked Ray

"I have my mom and dad, both lawyers, and they have one criminal daughter—that's sitting in front of you." She giggled.

"How about yours?" she asked.

"I have a wife and a son and my parents, who are enjoying their retirement at their home," he answered.

"What does your wife do?" she asked.

"She looks after her family business whenever she feels like it, and my life, my adorable son Krishaan, is at a boarding school on a hill station; his maternal aunt stays there and visits him every week, and most of the stay-at-home weekends he spends with her." He answered and asked the waiter for a refill.

"Don't you visit him? And why boarding, if I may ask?"

"We visit him once a month, at times once in two months if we are really tied up," he said and continued.

"Reason being, my wife belongs to a political background. Due to some political rivalry, Krishaan was attacked; for his safety, we decided to send him to boarding school until his 10th." He said as he poured her glass with beer.

"That's a tough call! Don't you miss him?"

"Hmm," he shook his head with teary eyes.

"He'll come out strong, I'm sure." She consoled him.

"Let's talk about our office. I guess that's better." He flashed his dimples and chugged the beer.

They were down two glasses, but who stops at just two pints! And they ordered another.

He started to get calls from his friend.

"Yes, yes, I am on my way; no need to pick me up; I'm already on my way!" he said and hung up.

"Let's go?" she asked.

"I wish to have another, but yeah, some other time." He said.

This time she wanted to pay the bill, insisting that last time she was too drunk to even realise she got her car there. He argued and gave his card.

The temperature in the atmosphere dropped significantly, and clouds were thundering, signalling it's going to rain cats and dogs. She rushed inside her car; he told her he'd drive and drop her first and return her car the next day.

The GPS indicated that the usual road with the flyover towards her house was jammed; hence they decided to take another lesser-driven route. Two minutes after they started, it started to rain heavily. He turned the heater on. Ten minutes later her car broke down on an isolated road surrounded with trees on both sides and no humans around.

"Shit! What happened?" She panicked.

"Hey, don't worry. Let the rain stop; I will check." He tried to infuse some courage in her.

His phone rang; it was his wife. He just saw her, and she nodded; she understood she didn't have to make any noise.

"Yes, I will do that. Yes, I know. Ok. Bye." He said and hung up.

She was literally trembling; suddenly the thoughts of this getting in light made her tense.

"Hey! It's alright; the rain will stop. Don't worry," he said.

"It's not about the rains…."

"Whatever it is, don't worry." He said and kept his hand on her shaking hand.

She felt at peace instantly.

"What if someone from the office sees us?" He asked.

"What! Where! Don't tell me!" She was agitated.

"Calm down. Do you think we are doing something forbidden?" he asked.

"What! No!" She answered.

"Then?"

"You know how the world is right, ever judging!" There was sadness in her voice.

"You got the point: the world will be like this, ever judging! So why worry? Moreover, we're not doing anything wrong!" He asserted.

"Yeah! We're not," she affirmed. Both doubted in their head what they just said.

The rain seemed to slow down, and he opened the bonnet and checked. The clutch cables were broken, which means they had to call a mechanic.

He called one of the mechanics he knew; he said he would be there in an hour due to traffic.

Arannya asked him to take a cab and go, and he made her realise how dumb she sounded. How could he leave her there alone and go? And he did not want her to take the cab as she was drunk.

So the best they could make out of the situation was to play nice music on the radio and talk.

The Darkhaast song blended seamlessly with the ambience.

"Such a beautiful song," he complimented.

"Indeed," she added, "Let's talk."

"Yeah," he shook his head.

"Let's talk about ourselves," he said.

"That's a difficult one!"

And they finally talked for real this time.

Their likes, dislikes, favourite movies, actors, music bands, composers, favourite colour, type of cuisine, best place they ever visited for a vacation, their favourite childhood memory, the type of clothing they liked, and talked about social media and extinct species, and what their ideal retirement life is. Etc. Arannya said when she gets old, she would want to live in a home mostly made of wood, a small and cosy place with a big garden and front yard. She wants to settle down in a city where it has the best of both worlds, like the ocean on one side and hills on the other and the city in between. Ray smiled at this, and she asked, What's funny? He shook his head. When she asked Ray about his ideal retirement life, he said he'd want to fast forward these 20 years and wake up old and fragile, sitting on a long and relaxing armchair made from the nicest African blackwood, and have someone at his disposal who he can share his life stories with, the ones that are deep hidden in his heart.

That hour passed swiftly, and the mechanic arrived.

One thing was clear between both of them. They were attracted to each other. From Ray's point of view, he was wrong, but he did not feel it that way in his heart; from Arannya's point of view, she was wrong too, but nothing in her life ever felt so right! It was mind vs. heart, and they both let the heart win.

They were soulmates, with a missed opportunity born over a decade apart; they could have been like a dream couple; alas, this can never happen in this lifetime. It was as if they were attached by an invisible string that kept pulling them towards one another. More than the grief of not being able to be with each other, to love each other openly ever, they were happy to experience this beautiful feeling, even for a short span of time, where they loved each other without any conditions, expectations, or bondage, with no pressure to even express their feelings to each other and just know what the other person feels about you. Isn't this true love in the actual sense?

This was like a spiritual crisis for them. Arannya, though younger than Ray, was a grown lady and had all the sense of what is right and what is wrong. Ray was expected to do the right thing given his age and experience; none were to be blamed for the emotions they were feeling towards each other. Maybe they really were meant to be, and due to the glitch in the matrix, they just were born in a separate timeline! What followed next was the time of their life. They did not even anticipate that their life was going to give them a fair and square chance at love, only if they both were courageous enough to think outside of the societal boundaries. Even before they realise their souls were already intertwined with each other.

This was maybe the first time when Arannya felt so calm and safe and good. Like there were no second thoughts, no inhibitions, she was feeling alive and happy. She was looking forward to Monday, which she once hated! Love has the power to make you like the things you thought you'd hate till your grave. She was experiencing a potpourri of emotions, making it difficult for her not to make it so obvious. Given her nature, she wasn't really comfortable sharing about her life, but this time there were so many butterflies in her stomach that she had to let her feelings out.

Laxmi observed her and asked what was happening and if she had finally given in to Gautam.

"No! I mean, he is a darling, but no!" Arannya smiled as she applied butter to her toast.

"Oh come on, Akka! Don't be so hard on him; he keeps talking about you, and most of the time when he is calling me, it's about you. At least reply to his messages, please," Laxmi said and asked her if she could make a toast for her too with jam added.

"I usually do, but at times I will read his text, mentally respond to it, and lock the phone. After an hour I will realise, Shit, I did not text him, and by the time I realise this, it's already too late to reply."

"By the way, Lax, I wanted to share something with you," she said.

"This sounds interesting!" Lax suddenly became excited and straightened her posture.

"So, there's this person in my office, and I think I am attracted to him."

"Who is the lucky guy!" Lax literally screamed.

"I mean, I think it may be just infatuation, or it's just attraction. Like, two people can like each other, right?" Arannya tried to say this with a convincing tone.

"Whoa, whoa, whoa, don't tell me you have fallen for a married man!" Laxmi said casually as she bit her slice.

"Not at all!" Arannya quickly retracted and thought for a second that even though she is close to Lax, she still feared being judged by someone younger than her.

"Okay! So tell me who he is." Lax enquired.

"Hmm, I'll tell you when the time is right." Arannya said and caressed Lax's hair.

"What? Akka, this is cruelty!" Lax made a frowning face.

"What else do you expect from Cruella!! Ha ha ha." Arannya acted cool and curtailed the conversation to save herself from being the subject of castigation.

She had to cool her excitement down and confine it within herself. But then she remembers she has had one person constant in her life since childhood, the one she would always turn to if she was just lost in her life, and the person would do the same. It was like they'd not know too many details about each other's lives but just the important events and happenings in, say, bullet points, but whenever they'd connect, they'd pick up the topic they'd last discussed, even if it was months apart. And that person was Shiney.

Arannya finished her breakfast and ran to her room to dial her.

God knows what her caller tune was, but it was killing the hell out of Arannya's ears.

Shiney answered the call, "Think of the Devil! I was supposed to call you today!"

"Oh, shut up! First of all, what kind of caller tune is this? Change it!"

"No, sorry, I won't! This keeps me saved from my manager, who used to call me 10 times a day for silly things! Bloody motherfucker! Since I kept this, he hates to call me now," Shiney said, and they both burst into laughter.

"Where are you fucking around these days, you bitch! Do you even realise it's been more than six fucking months since we spoke?" Shiney cussed.

"Well, I reciprocate the same, you asshole! My phone did not buzz with your calls or messages either." Arannya faked a snobbish tone.

"Yeah, yeah! Sorry about that. By the way, I have changed my previous job and moved to the Northeast; things have been really hectic in my current org, but somehow I think I am settling in." Shiney continued.

"You tell me. How are things? Are you still a virgin lady or did you finally do some justice to that little rose down there?" Shiney asked.

"Stop it, Shiney, early morning don't induce such sinful thoughts in me!" Arannya warned.

"My Virgin Lady!" Shiney teased.

"Hey, you said you were supposed to call me? What was that regarding?" Arannya asked.

"Oh yes! I will be coming to your city this week; there's some seminar that I am supposed to attend."

"What! That's amazing news! Don't worry; I will arrange everything here at my place."

"I am not sure if I'd be able to stay because I will reach there on Tuesday, and then it's a three-day-long seminar. I will have to be at my company's arranged accommodations. I mean, why not take full advantage of this? Anyway, so on Friday these people planned to explore the city, but I have told them that I will be visiting you, and then on the same day we have a late-night flight. This way we'd get an entire day, if it is possible for you to take leave. Which I am sure you can, because Miss Aarna, who feels proud to get a 100% attendance even in her workplace, will definitely have tons of leaves in her bucket!"

Shiney spoke in one breath.

"Yeah! At your service, ma'am." Arannya agreed.

"And why did you call?" Shiny asked.

"Oh, it's nothing; we'll talk once you are here."

"I know it's not "Nothing", but anyway, let's meet and discuss. See you soon. Love you."

"Love you too, bye."

In the evening, Lax planned for a house party, and of course, Gautam's love towards Arannya was the catalyst. Since Arannya had nothing planned but to replay the time in the car with Ray in her head, she agreed to join them. Lax requested Arannya prepare her signature lasagna with the typical pickle taste and some prawn fry.

Gautam arrived at 4 pm for an evening party on the pretext of helping the girls.

And Lax did not even shy away from asking him to clean the living room and set it up.

"Umm, I am good with the cooking, actually." He said Lax and begged with folded hands to let him help Arannya in the kitchen.

"Huh! Of course!" Lax smirked and pulled the linen off the sofa.

"Akka, your assistant has changed!" She mocked her.

Arannya, who is in her own world with beautiful thoughts about Ray and the amazing feeling, is continually blushing and flirting back with Gautam. When you are in love, you don't want to hurt anyone in any manner; in fact, when Gautam smashed the fridge door, she was like, "Easy, baby! Oh, that poor thing!"

Hearing that, Gautam repeated the same action, "Tch." Aarnnya narrowed her eyes and looked at him.

"Say it," a curious Gautam looked at her.

"Say what?"

"Easy, baby!" He sounded cheesy.

"Duh!!" She hit him with the carrot.

"Oh my God! Is there oxytocin in that wine of yours?" He pointed to her glass.

"Check for yourself." She winked, handed the glass to him, removed her apron, and went to get a shower.

Gautam was having the time of his life. He looked for Lax, who was already watching this sitcom from her slant eye, "What's happening?" Gautam mouthed. "I don't know!" Lax mouthed back and was like, "Why are we talking like this?" she said and turned the music system on.

It was 7 pm, and Cahitra, Emraan, and Daniel came with crates of beer and whisky.

This time they resorted to old-school games and ditched UNO for charades.

Since Rishi went for his coding classes, he did not come. So they made two teams based on genders.

The game started; Emraan gave Arannya the movie name; she mimicked it by waving goodbye, making an action of "No" like a teacher from her index finger, and making an action from her hand like waves coming out of her mouth, which implies saying something.

These two drunk girls were breaking their heads trying to make sense out of it.

"Goodbye, No, Sing? Goodbye, no sing?" Chaitra was guessing, "It is a Hindi movie, Chaits!" Lax scolded her.

"Bye mat kaho? Chaitra guessed again! "Drop it already; let me try." Lax gets competitive when it comes to games.

"Bye means Alvida, mat, kaho?" Lax tried to get the movie name.

Arannya gave her a thumbs up that she got one word correct, and she kept waving goodbye, making an action of "No" like a teacher from her index finger and making an action from her hand like waves coming out of her mouth. It was almost like a dance step, and the boys were having a ball, laughing their arse off.

Then Arannya mimicked Amitabh Bachan's iconic "Haay" gesture of asking 'what' with her right hand and left hand on her waist; Lax gets it that the movie has Amitabh Bacchan, and then Arannya does Sharukh Khan's signature move of spreading his arms.

"Oh, okay, so the film has both Amitabh and SRK!"

"Alvida... Alvidaaa" Lax was trying her best to get the name.

"Tick tick 1, tick tick 2," the boys began the countdown.

"Kabhi hulvida na kehna," Chaitra said in her native accent.

"Phew! Thank God!" Arannya sighed.

Now it was Girls turn to give the name, and Lax whispered it in Gautam's ears.

For a nice 3 minutes he did not even come up with what exactly to do so that he drops hints and clues. Then he started to point at Arannya. The guys scratched their heads and tried to make some sense out of it. But all Gautam did was to point her.

"We give up, we give up!" Emraan surrendered.

"Yay! We won, we won!" Lax leaped with joy.

Even Arannya and Chaitra did not know what the movie name was.

"Yeah, yeah! Now give us the damn movie name!" Daniel said.

"Mere Mehboob," Gautam said and blushed like a newlywed bride, only to get trashed by the guys brutally later.

It was 12:30 am, and Chaitra was supposed to sleep in Lax's room with her, and the boys in the living room. Lax was sloshed, and Arannya helped her get up and took her to her room. "How much have you had on the rocks, Lax? At least you could have eaten something filling." she said. "I love you, Akka," the inevitable dialogue of every drunk girl to another girl who is around her.

"Yeah, I know."

"No, really, I love you, and I pray for all the happiness in the world for you." Laxmi said as she adjusted herself on the bed, Arannya pulled the blanket for her and turned the AC on.

Lax held her hand and said something that she wasn't expecting at all.

"It doesn't matter, Akka! ....." she blabbered. Arannya asked, "What doesn't?"

"It doesn't matter if you have fallen for a married man; if you are happy, I would bloody kidnap him for you, trust me." Arannya got a lump in her throat by hearing this; how can someone so much younger than her show such a level of boldness?

"Laxmi, sleep now. Good night."

Sunday slipped away quickly with Arannya's self-care regime. All she thought on Sunday was about the next day. She ditched the bright colour for a Monday and chose to wear a jet black kurti with a multicolour dupatta, pairing it with her silver danglers and Kolhapuri chappals. Lax gave her a "I know for whom you're doing all this" look.

She blushed and headed to the office.

During lunchtime, Sujith announced that his team and a few members from Arannya's team, like Samar, Pooja, and Shweta, and some HRs are planning for a weekend trip this week. They have booked an entire resort and will start right after the office on Friday; the place is a 6-hour drive. Arannya, who was sitting opposite Ray, was quiet. Today the place next to Ray was already occupied by Sharanya, who was the HR, and her liking towards Ray was an open secret; only Arannya wasn't aware until Sujith told her.

"I'm very excited; I hope I can tag along with you, Ray," Sharanya said.

"Hmm, yeah, sure," Ray obliged, making Arannya fussing with jealousy and anger.

"What about you, Aaru? If you don't wish to drive all the way, then I can be your chauffeur." Sujith, who was sitting next to her, said this and winked in an attempt to make Ray jealous. Arannya played along, "Oh, I'd love that! But unfortunately I won't be able to make it," she said and looked at Ray's reaction; he tried to act cool, but his whining was evident.

"No! Please don't do that. You have to come." Sujith insisted.

"Why?" Ray asked and made eye contact with her.

"My friend is visiting me, so I'd be on leave on Friday, hence,"

"Can't it be postponed?" Sujith asked.

"Not a chance," she said and got up from the table to wash her hands.

Ray went behind her. While washing his hands, he asked, "Try if you can."

"Why? Anyway, you have a nice company, right? I am sure you guys will have a lot of fun!" She sounded pissed. And she walked off. She realised quickly that she overdid it.

But once an arrow is shot, it doesn't come back.

This wasn't a great week in terms of emotions for her; she was premenstrual and was getting irked by every little discomfort. She managed not to indulge in any conversation with Ray to avoid any misunderstanding and heated conversation.

She resorted to one-word answers.

"How are you? Ray would ask.

"Good," she would reply.

"What time are you leaving home?" he would ask.

"8," she would answer.

"Is it fixed that you won't come?" He would enquire.

"Yes," she would affirm.

Even Sujith, who was an onlooker, got irritated.

"Leave her be, Ray; after lunch, let's plan the itinerary," Sujith said.

"Yeah, okay," Ray agreed.

That week went by quicker than usual, and it was already Thursday.

During the lunch hour, Sujith was exaggerating about how beautiful that resort is, surrounded by forest and mesmerising, breathtaking views of the hills in the distance.

"See, Arannya, we still have a spot left, in case you change your mind," he mocked her.

"I wish, but I have already made the plans. Moreover, she has a late-night flight at 1:30 am, so I'll have to drop her off too," she said.

The next day, Arannya went near the hotel where Shiney was staying. She asked her to take all her luggage as she will drop her to the airport directly from her place.

She was waiting in the lobby for her, and as soon as Shiney came out of the lift, she ran towards her screaming. "Aaruuuuuuuuuu," and hugged her.

"Oh my God, you haven't changed a bit," Shiney said.

"Neither have you!" She replied.

She drove her to her place and asked if she wanted to eat something out or go shopping, etc. Shiney said she just wants to be home, sip wine, and do the thing they were best at: "gossiping"!

After a 45-minute drive, they reached her place.

"This is such a nice place, Aaru," said Shiney, as she was really impressed to see her apartment.

"Wait until you see the balcony," Arannya said and slid the door open to the balcony.

"Oh my god, I can sit here all day sipping wine and reading books,"

"You want me to get the bottle here?"

"You read my mind!" Shiney exclaimed.

"Cool, make yourself comfortable."

"Goes without saying," Shiney said and spread her body across the chaise lounge.

"I wish I would have stayed here," she said to Arannya.

"I told you." Arannya came and pulled another chaise lounge near her and kept a small table between them with some nachos and mayonnaise.

She poured the wine and they cheered.

"So, tell me, what was it that you wanted to tell me the other day?" Shiney asked.

"Let the wine reach my stomach at least," Arannya pleaded.

"Yeah, yeah, take your time." Shiney said and continued, "By the way, do you remember Vishal?"

"Vishal? Who?" Arannya was clueless.

"Vishal, our schoolmate Ruby's boyfriend?" Shiney tried to make her remember.

"Vishal... Oh yes, Rooh and Wish! Hahaha, what about him?" Arannya sipped her wine and munched the nachos.

"He is also working in the same company as I; in fact, he too is here for the conference."

"Oh, that's nice."

"He wanted to meet you," Shiney sounded fishy.

"What?" Arannya gulped the wine. "Why?" she asked.

"I don't know. I told him that I'll be meeting you, so he asked if it is possible for him to meet you too. Since this happened only when I was checking out, I told him anyway you will be dropping me off at the airport so he can meet you there." Shiney said.

"Okay, yeah, whatever. Now listen to what I wanted to say." Arannya completely ignored Vishal's topic and got into the mood of pouring her heart out as the third glass of wine hit her soul.

"So..." she began, from the night where they first exchanged the words at the office party and gave her every detail about what happened and how she feels so good around him and how she doesn't feel anything wrong while she knows that even if they haven't crossed any boundaries, it doesn't mean they are totally right about this.

Shiney heard her without interrupting.

"So what do you think this is? Am I doing something wrong?" Arannya asked.

Shiney finished the last sip of her wine and said, "Aaru, there is no absolute right or absolute wrong in this world. It's all very subjective." to Arannya's disappointment, for the first time she wasn't expecting her to be diplomatic.

"Drop the diplomacy, arsehole, and tell me if this is wrong." Arannya fired back.

"Like I said, Aaru, it's a very subjective matter; we don't know in what circumstances he is in or what his intentions are towards this. As far as you are concerned, I would suggest that you don't get emotionally attached. I have seen you going through some real shit, and I don't want to see you in that position again. Go be with him, fuck around for that matter, but you always have to keep one thing in mind: "He already belongs to someone else," and you should be ready to bear the infamy it will cause you if this thing comes to light. As for me, I will always be by your side in whatever decision you make, but remember that you have your life too; you will be getting married to someone sooner or later. That time this thing should never be a hindrance in any manner."

"Hmm, yeah." Shiney's words ran a shiver down Arannya's spine.

It was as if she got knocked on her head and suddenly woke up to reality. A sense of guilt started to fill her up, and she became all dull and silent.

"Hey! Hey, drama queen! Chill! It's okay; everything is fine. Don't think too much. All I wanted to say is, "Just have fun and don't get hurt, baby!" Shiney said and hugged her.

She hugged her back. Arannya treated her with her signature lasagna with pickle taste, which Shiney rejected outright.

The rest of the time they spoke about visiting their hometown during the festival and planning to meet old buddies. Shiney made sure she didn't bring up Kartik's topic.

It was 8 P.M., and they had to leave for the airport as it was a 2-hour drive.

"Are you sure you'd be okay driving Aaru?"

"Yes, I will, I think."

"I don't think so. I think I should just take the cab and go."

"Are you mad! No! I will drop you."

"Hmmm, then we'll take the cab only. This way we don't have to worry about driving."

"Sounds good." Said Arannya, who was actually tipsy and praised Shiney for her intellect.

They reached the airport around 10 and checked into a lounge called "Buffalo Fire Wings."

"Have you been here before?" asked Shiney.

"Mostly when I have a flight, I will kill an hour here and then check in."

"Such nice and cosy vibes." Shiney sighed.

"What do we order?" Arannya went through the menu and asked.

"A beer would be fine, I think, and chicken wings," Shiney said.

"Hmm, perfect!"

After they finished a pint, Shiney asked if she could call Vishal there.

"Vishal? Oh yes, yeah, call him."

Some 15 minutes later he came and greeted both of them and hugged Arannya.

"Oh my God, you guys are smelling like one of those cheap bars!"

"Desi Daru Theka!" Shiney said and chugged her beer.

"Arannya! So good to see you, man!"

"Likewise," she smiled.

"Would you mind stepping out with me for some time?" he asked.

"Shiney, please excuse us," he said.

Arannya with a confused face saw Shiney. Shiney gave her a nod.

They came out in the balcony section.

"Do you want one?" asked Vishal as he lit his cigarette.

"No thanks, I don't."

"Knock some sense into Shiney; she beats me when it comes to smoking!"

"Does she! She told me she came down to two cigarettes per day!"

"Haha, per hour she meant," he clarified.

"Without beating around the bush, let me come straight to the point." Vishal said and kneeled down.

Arannya was amazed.

"I'm so, so, so sorry, Arannya; I have sinned. I have wronged you. I am unable to forgive myself. I beg your pardon; please forgive me; please accept my apologies." He said and hung his head low.

"Wait! What is happening? I don't understand! And please get up; you are creating a scene here," she requested.

"First promise me that you will accept my apologies and forgive me." Vishal pleaded.

"Okay, fine, even though I don't know what this is about, I will forgive you."

"No, say that you forgive me, please."

"Oh God! Yeah, okay, I forgive you. Now get your ass up."

He got up and hugged her. He almost squeezed her and wasn't ready to let go of her. Arannya noticed he was crying, and she tried to console him, "Hey, it's fine; don't cry." She patted his back.

He released her and wiped his tears.

"Are you alright?"

"Much better now, thanks to you,"

"Now tell me what this was about, because I guess there is some huge misunderstanding here, since I don't remember anything in my life that has to do with you."

"There is Arannya, there is." He was pensive.

He made her sit on the chair, held her hands, and said, "Please listen to me with an open mind and a generous heart."

"Oh my God, cut the crap and get to the point, Vishal! You're scaring the shit out of me now!" She got furious.

"Okay, let's do this." He said and looked up in the sky as if asking for courage from God.

"You remember our last exam from class 6th? It was a drawing paper."

"Yes, I think I remember." She was now intrigued.

"That day after the exam got over, Sajan had to leave early for his home, but he wanted to meet you, so he waited for you like 10 minutes, but you were still in the classroom, and his uncle was waiting for him outside the school."

As soon as she heard Sajan's name, she got the chills. What now? She wondered, still she held herself together and maintained a calm demeanour.

"Yeah, he must be wanting to take his sketch pens back," she said.

"I am not sure of that, but that day he asked me to give you the message that he will be waiting for you at the

'Bunny Bun' bakery at 4 pm. But somehow it slipped from my mind."

He continued, "I went home around 7:30 pm, and my mom told me that Sajan had called multiple times asking if I was home. I got scared. I knew I screwed up! But till this moment I was still a human; what happened next made me a monster," he said and stopped.

"What next? Tell me." She raised her voice.

"I got a call from him again; he asked, 'Bro, where were you? Did you tell Arannya that I am waiting for her?' 'Bro, are you still there?' I asked. 'Yes, I am! I have to meet her.' Sajan replied.

'But I told her to meet you; honestly, dude, she did not seem interested and behaved like a bitch, saying, 'Better luck next time?'"

Arannya got up abruptly and screamed, "You motherfucking monster!!!! You've ruined my life!!!"

"Just fuck off from here, or else I will kill you!!!"

Hearing the commotion, Shiney rushed out.

"Oh my God, what happened, guys?"

"This motherfucker ruined my life, Shiney. If it were not for this arsehole, I'd have been happily married and having kids right now with Sajan." Arannya grinned and clenched her fists.

"What! Okay, alright, I know this fucker did screw up, but that doesn't mean you'd have had a life with him." Shiney said.

"What do you mean, how can you be so sure? And don't you tell me that you were aware all this while!" Arannya fumed.

"I only learnt about this today, Aaru," Shiney assured her.

Shiney opened her Facebook and showed Sajan's profile, which was named "Sa Jaan." He came out openly as gay and is living his best life with his African partner in Australia.

"Huh!" Arannya laughed at her fate; what an utterly tragic novel her life has been! Who has written the story of her life, she wondered.

Vishal was waiting quietly to be forgiven.

"Okay, let bygones be bygones. I don't have any grudge against you, but I don't understand what made you confess this to me now. You could have kept this to yourself." Arannya checked the time, and asked the waiter to get the check.

"The thing is, none of my relationships worked out, and one day I was thinking what sin have I committed, then I got reminded of this day, and I searched for Sajan to confess, but when I saw that he turned out to be gay, I consoled myself into thinking that it eventually turned out in your interest!" confessed Vishal.

"Oh! Thank you so much! That was really thoughtful of you! But that doesn't mean your future relations will work out!" Arannya mocked.

"Duh! I should've kept it to myself. It was just a peccadillo," he grinned.

"Guys, it's 12; I think you guys should leave now," she said, and they walked out of the lounge.

They hugged each other, and Arannya tapped hard on Vishal's head, asking him not to think on this part now and be free from guilt because she is very happy wherever she is in her life.

"Yes, Vishal! She got the 'Ray' of hope in her life. Don't you worry." Shiney winked, and they both went inside the airport.

Arannya lost track of her phone; she unlocked it and saw 7 missed calls from Ray. She immediately called him back, "Hey, hi! Sorry, my phone was in my bag, and it was on silent mode."

"Hi, no worries! Where are you now?"

"I am at the airport, will book the cab and go home now. What about you guys? Did you reach the resort?"

"No, actually I got some work back at home, so I asked them to carry on, and I would join them later. By the way, I am at the airport. If you come near exit 3, it's just a 4-hour drive from here; we can reach there by 5."

"What? But I didn't get any clothes, etc."

"That can be managed. Hurry up now; we are already late!" He said and hung up.

She literally ran toward exit no. 3, as if she had to obey whatever Ray would tell her. She was jumping with happiness. It was like a dream she never even dared to dream about.

Herself and him, on a long, wonderful drive. She would have never thought about it, but then the Universe has its own course and surprises for special souls like theirs. The entire spiritual force was working its best to make these two souls meet and make them realise that they belong together. It was as if in the cosmic conference the prime project was to make 'Ray and Arannya fall for each other.'

"Hi!" She said as she tried to catch her breath.

"Hey, Hope, you had a good time with your friend," he asked as he opened the door for her.

"Yeah! It was amazing. I got to meet one more friend of ours, Vishal, that arsehole! Oops," she said and covered her mouth.

"What did he do to deserve this? Is he your ex?"

"What? No, but he is the potential reason that my first love never worked out. Haha, long story; I will give you the details along the way."

"Well, doesn't that mean he is somewhere the reason that we met?" He asked.

"Come to think of it, yes. I should just forgive him." She giggled.

"Buckle up, Arannya. Let's hit the road!" Ray said enthusiastically.

Were they not thinking straight, or were they not thinking anything at all? Whatever it was, they had no inhibitions about this. Ray turned up the music volume. *'Tose naina laage piya saawre,'* the song sounded like magic.

Both of them were living the life they secretly wished for, and the angels above were orchestrating moments like this exotically. They both knew this was something special, but were waiting for another to take the lead.

Then there was a moment when their eyes made contact, and they saw each other without blinking for a minute until another vehicle passed by. It was the moment when they spoke a thousand words; all the unspoken emotions from their hearts were conveyed. How badly they needed each other, how they felt complete with each other, how if given a chance they would escape from this world and make a new world for themselves. How they will be beside each other when they grow old. It was the moment they thought that even if death came to take them, they'd happily die being beside each other.

The weather became sinful, and it started to rain; the meteorological report turned out to be a fallacy again. The romantic songs were adding fuel to the inflammable chemistry between them.

"Baahon ke darmiyaan, do pyaar mil rahe hain.

Jaane kya bole mann, Dole sunke badan

Dhadkan bani zubaan"

This song from her childhood crush Salman Khan's movie gave them the momentum to feel the waves flowing between them, dive into each other's energy, and surrender to the sensual moment. It was the need of the hour when they embraced each other, but the social conditioning was fighting strong, and they both held themselves back.

Since Arannya was tipsy, she thought, Let's blame it on the sweet alcohol again. She slid her hand towards the gear stick in an attempt to touch his hand. But, as soon as he was about to change the gear, she retracted. She attempted this enough times for Ray to realise, and he finally said, "It's okay; you can hold my hand."

Embarrassed but riding on the guilty pleasure, she took her hand, overlapped it on his, which was holding the gear stick, and enclosed it. She closed her eyes and felt like she got connected to her missing puzzle. After a while, Ray turned his hand around and intertwined his fingers with hers. And pulled her hand towards him and kept it on his thighs. Arannya was going crazy; whatever was happening, she just didn't want this to get over; the rains on top of it made the hormones in her body run wild.

Arannya tightened the grip of her hand; what Ray did next made her lose herself. He took her hand and planted a sensual kiss with his soft, cottony lips.

He didn't ask for her permission; she didn't mind it either. They did not exchange a word, yet their silence said it all.

This was the moment they realised, 'They were in love.'

Twas 5 am in the morning, and Arannya was fast asleep. Ray reached the destination, turned the car off, and googled at her with admiration. Saw how this white soul is so special in many different ways. She is a great friend, a great daughter, and an amazing person when it comes to work. How on earth this girl remained unloved he wondered. He dialled Sujith and asked him to arrange a room for her.

"Arannya? Aaru?" He tried waking her up, but there she was, a sleeping beauty slumbering in her own world, drooling. Ray turned her face towards him and wiped her mouth with his hand; she opened her eyes slowly with his touch, saw him, and held him by his arms to sleep again as though she was dreaming. Ray caressed her hair, and suddenly startled, "Oh Sujith," she jumped like a frog hearing that. "What! Where?" and he laughed. "That's satanic!" she smirked. In another minute, Sujith came and nudged her, "Get up, Miss. Your personal butler is at your service!"

"Get some rest. We'll meet at breakfast." Ray said and walked out of the car.

Around 8 am, Arannya's sleep broke, and she saw there was a T-shirt and shorts kept on the table. With a note, Ray has sent: "Please change and come for breakfast". It was his T-shirt and shorts, and luckily it fit her well. It was like she mistakenly traversed into a parallel world.

Everything was dreamy. Heavenly!

In the dining area, most of them finished their breakfast and were sipping coffee. Her eyes were searching for him; there he was, busy talking to the local driver and asking about the places to explore. Look at him, she thought, such a mature and reliable person. Everyone looks up to him and listens to him. He is so perfect. Like Johnny Bravo. She can just blindly trust him; in fact, she slept peacefully beside him in the car knowing that nothing can go wrong if he is beside her.

Ray, for a man, was far better than her imagination. Surreal.

"Okay everyone, get ready soon; we'll be leaving in an hour." Ray instructed everyone. Arannya was still eating her breakfast when Sharanya came to her and asked, "When do you come?"

"Early morning, Ray got me here!" She threw a fake smile and had so much pride in her eyes while she said that, specifically to make her jealous. And she nailed it. Sharanya gave her an awful look.

Ray was observing her and smiled at her theatrics. After most people left to get ready, Arannya took two cups of coffee and waited for Ray to come. "So thoughtful, thank you," he said.

"Hope you got enough rest?" he asked.

"Yes, I did, thank you."

"What's with that face?" Ray asked after receiving her gloomy response.

"Everyone will wear fresh, nice clothes; I will have to repeat," she frowned.

"It's okay; I know you can manage for a day." He said casually and asked her to get ready quickly.

This behaviour of his was screwing with her head. At times he is so sensual and romantic, and the next day suddenly he will act as if nothing ever happened. This wishy-washy behaviour of Ray, instead of putting her emotions off, was making her even more attracted towards him.

They all set out to explore the little hill station. Most of the time Ray and Sujith were busy managing the trip; she tagged along with the girls group, but she didn't miss a chance to steal a glance of him whenever she could. They went for a small uphill trek, but since she already had a long, tiring day the previous night, her energy levels went low, and she decided to go back from the middle of the trek.

"Huh, phew! Sujith, I can't walk a step further," she was gasping.

"What!? You know what they call a person who abandons the troupe? Fugitive!" Sujith tried to convince her by making her feel pathetic about herself.

"Oh please, none of this can make me move an inch. I'm going back; can you please ask Ray for his car keys?" she asked.

"Why only the keys? Should I ask him to join you too?" Sujith winked and teased her.

She picked the pebble from the ground and pelted it at him; her target was spot on.

"Ouch! I can sue you for this, Madam," he threatened jokingly.

"Go ahead!" She said and sat at one of the cornerstones.

"Wait up; I'll get the keys from him." He ran panting upwards to Ray.

After a few minutes, she saw Ray walking towards her. She was really in a dishevelled state and didn't wish him to see her in such a state, with frizzy hair and sweat all over.

"Why did that idiot bother you? I'm so sorry." She was evidently guilty.

"Don't be bothered; in fact, I'm a little exhausted too. I used your tiredness as an escape. So I owe you one." He smiled and extended his hands to her, who was struggling to get up.

"Welcome to old age," he ridiculed.

"Oh! Please! It's just that I'm tired; otherwise I have the stamina to scale the Himalayas," she replied. "I see that!" He laughed it off.

"Honestly, you missed some amazing views up there." She said as she sat in the car.

"Not really!" He said and gazed at her, making steady eye contact for 6 seconds. She got a little awkward. "ready to roll?" he asked and pulled her seat belt to buckle it.

"Where are we going? These people will come," she said.

"It's going to take another 2 hours for them. Don't worry; you won't regret this," he winked.

He drove her across the small village. Beautiful trails of flowers on both sides of the road, and the paths often less walked upon, made it resemble the street in Auvers-sur-

Oise. He parked his car aside, and they went for a walk. There was a local bakery that was baking some delicious bread. "Hungry?" he asked. "Not really," she replied, not to look ravenous. Still he went and brought cream buns for her. Could this get any better? She thanked the Universe for this time, which she is going to cherish forever. "Now let's go buy some clothes for you," he said and held her hand. As they walked in the market, they felt like the world around them had turned pink. Everything was so alluring. The florist, the chaiwala, kids walking holding their moms sarees, a person selling goggles at 100 rs. The water bubbles that were blown by the kids made it look like straight out of a Bollywood flick, only a song was missing, which was then covered by a person selling the flutes. They bought two kurtis, both Ray chose for her, and the bindi, of course, of the water droplet shape.

It was night, and a bonfire was set up in the garden area. Everyone gathered around; the girls wore nice dresses, and Arannya was the happiest wearing the clothes bought by him. One of the females asked if she wanted to try one of her outfits, but she declined politely. The party started; everyone was tired from trekking.

The resort caretaker arranged a woodfire in the garden area for them. After having a few pegs, they cracked jokes, sang songs, and danced on the current chartbusters. Arannya and Ray, sitting across from each other, were thinking of the time they drank together. Both of them wanted to get aside and drink, but alas, the decorum. Everyone was drinking like a fish. Both of them had just one peg, as they knew after a while these people would be sloshed. This was the strategy they implemented without even discussing it. The chemistry between them was adamantine, and they were in perfect sync with each other.

Then each one of them had to showcase their talents. Arannya, who was barely good at anything but cooking lasagna, thought, What could she possibly show? So she waited till everyone's turn came. Most of them sang, few danced, Sujith did beatboxing, and Sharanya recited some ghazals. It was Ray's turn. But he insisted Arannya take it.

"I'm good at cooking lasagne; there's nothing I can showcase here. Sorry for the disappointment," she said and bowed.

"The way you exist is your talent, Arannya. Arannya, everyone!" Samar said and clapped, followed by others. She was filled with pride and gratification.

"Okay, so I used to write in my college days." Ray said. Everyone started to hoot.

"Not a great one, but recently I have written a few lines, if I may?" He asked.

"Yay! Ray Go ahead!" they said in unison.

"Uh-huh, uh-huh," he cleared his throat, looked at Arannya, and said,

"When I catch you looking at me,

I wonder how it could be?

Time stops, and so do we.

and the realm is only me and thee."

The audiences broke into amusement and claps. And she knew it was written for her.

It was 2 am, and half of them were knocked off, and the other half took the others to their respective rooms. Samar offered to escort Arannya to her room; she said she would have a couple of drinks more. Samar insisted on sticking with her, but he was so drunk that he couldn't even stand properly; another person came and took him inside.

At last, it was just the two of them. Ray asked her to wait, went inside, and bought her favourite whisky. She was delighted with that.

"What are you trying to do?" she asked him in a sceptical tone.

"What do you mean?" he asked.

"Don't act innocent; it's just the two of us now." She said and pulled an empty chair next to her for him to sit.

"Is it some kind of warning?" He flashed his dimples and offered her the peg.

"So?" he asked.

"So?" She mimicked.

"How is your trip going, Aarna?"

"Was that a freudian slip, or did you just call me Aarna?"

"I have overheard you when one day you were talking over a phone call saying, 'This is Aarna, Aarna."

"Someone possesses an acute hearing sense," she said.

"And someone is possessive." He mocked her. She made a duck face, he pulled her cheeks, and she turned red like a cherry.

That night they didn't speak; their eyes did all the talking. Their bodies were talking to each other. They exchanged glances after glances and sipped glasses after glasses. He helped her put her hair strands behind her ear; she wiped the chips granule from his lips. Then there came a moment when they both bent to pick up the bottle, and their faces came very close to each other, lips just a fingertip away. Both of them closed their eyes in an attempt to leave it to the moment, but then someone from the property walked past them and broke the momentum. They bounced back to reality quickly and exchanged shy glances.

The moment was on the verge of becoming awkward; Arannya took a deep breath and extended her hand towards him. He slid his finger, gliding from her wrist, and intertwined them tightly.

"We are not doing anything wrong, right?" She asked with a teary eye.

"Nothing could be more righteous than this," he said, pulling her closer and hugging her. They embraced each other warmly and tightly, feeling each other's body, breath, and heartbeats. It was so magnetic that they could feel the pull towards each other, like they wanted to get inside each other's body.

The world around them stopped; at this moment they did not care if someone came and saw them; nothing could come between the heavenly reunion of these two separated souls. The aura around them beaming with love made them realise this is not just another affair or a passing fancy but home to their souls. It was the true union of the divine feminine and the divine masculine. They were the knight and the queen, the emperor and the empress. They were past life lovers, fated to meet during this lifetime. Ill-fated to be born a decade apart.

The alma gemela.

The ones who have no clue why they are attracted to each other. But they yearn to be near each other. Gets pulled towards each other. If one person isn't in a good mood, the other will get to know about it. Call it telepathy or any fancy word, but they would just know if the other person needs them or is in trouble. Their connection was not obligatory of any words, conditions, or gestures; if need be, they'd happily give up their lives for each other. But this kind of bond wasn't made for this world; people could never understand the connection between them. They would call it lustful, illicit, immoral, shameful, and whatnot. But none of this mattered to them; they knew the purity of it, and this made them a greater human being at the end of it. The colour of their love wasn't red after all; it was white: pure and chaste.

Now begins a love story that has no predefined destination; they were living one day at a time. When they were near each other, they didn't want to be apart; in fact, the angels helped them catalyse their relationship when Ray's floor was due for renovation and they were shifted to Arannya's floor. This made them live the life of their dreams. The cranky mornings turned ecstatic. Going to the office was a blissful affair rather than a punishment. One entire week they decided to confuse people by twinning each day. But nobody really commented or noticed except for Sujith, who was now sure there was something brewing between these two. But he seemed to be genuinely happy for both of them. Sujith was the first person Arannya spoke to when she joined this office. And he was close to Ray like a little brother. It was a wonderful time for them; during lunch hour, they made sure they were sitting next to each other and used to hold hands under the table. People started to notice them, but instead of getting cautious, they both were enjoying all the attention. And then, their camaraderie caught the eyes of some office vultures who were never happy in anybody's happiness no matter what, and when it had a personal angle to it, they were bound to screw things up between the two of them. These were Sharanya, who had her eyes on Ray, and Dinesh, who had a history and a connection with Ray.

One day in the office, Arannya looked pale and unwell. Ray, who was now sitting next to her with an aisle dividing them, asked her to go home, but she wanted to stay in the office just to be around him. After a while, when she was coming back to her place, she got vertigo. Her blood pressure went low. Ray rushed and lifted her up, took her to the dormitory, and called the in-house doctor. People's eyes were gouged out looking at what just happened. When she regained consciousness, she found Ray and a few other colleagues around her. This episode has raised a lot of eyebrows, and it has become a hot topic in the office.

"Haven't I told you to go home? No more nonsense now. Meet me near the entrance. I am dropping you home." He ordered and dashed out of the room.

"Aaaru, be careful, man; you scared the hell out of us!" Sujith said and took her bag to drop her till the gate.

"Sorry for the scene; I don't know how I didn't keep track of my sugar intake," she said.

"Go home and rest now." Sujith said. *Beep beep*, Ray honked.

"I am sorry," she said as she sat in the car.

"Shove it up your ass!" Ray fired back.

The whole drive they didn't speak; Arannya was afraid to even utter a word. Ray kept a stoic face. It was only when he did not take a turn towards her place that she said, "You missed the turn." No response from him. After a while he stopped his car in front of a stand-alone building's gate and honked; a guard came out of the tiny room and opened the gate. She realised he had taken her to his place. "Is this your place?" she asked. "At least ask better questions." He gnashed his teeth. They came to the fourth floor, and there was just one house. "Narayan's" reads the nameplate with a small design of a deck chair. He pressed some four digits on the lock and opened the door.

Arannya was mesmerised to see his place; it was spick and span. The entire house was painted in dual tones of white and forest grey. Every corner of the house, every piece of furniture, small or large, was screaming of opulence. 'Beep,' the door made the sound as it got locked. She was just standing there in awe. Ray came in front of her and hugged her. "I got so scared," he said and hugged her tighter. She hugged him back. Still hypnotised by the beautiful house. Her eyes fell on a picture of him, his wife, and their child, and guilt filled her as quickly as some reflexive action. She retracted herself. He held her hand and made her sit on the sofa.

"Where is she?" she asked.

"At her hometown," he replied.

"Why did you bring me here?"

"Don't worry; I will drop you back if you want. You are not doing fine, and I just couldn't think of anything but to be near you and look after you. Be here for some time if you're comfortable," he requested.

She looked at his eyes and blinked slowly and smiled. It was a yes. He went into the kitchen, poured her a glass of beetroot juice, and served her avocado salad.

"Eat and drink this first," he ordered; she obeyed.

"What if the guard snitches on you?" she asked. "Doesn't she stay with you?" She was shooting questions after questions. He chose to keep quiet, and once she was done eating, he lifted her up and took her to a room.

It was his study. It had his computer, a big draughting table with sheets and reference images clipped to the board, and trace papers. It had a shelf filled with books, magazines, and even records. Yellow bean bags in the corner and a queen-size bed in the middle facing a large screen, connected to PlayStations and gaming joysticks.

"Wooh! This is something!" She was amused.

"The juxtaposition of work and play." he said and placed her on the bed.

"No more questions; you need to take a rest now. Sleep for some time."

"Stay by my side," she said and closed her eyes.

He pulled the bean bag and sat next to the bed; she opened her palms, and he slid his hand, gliding from her wrist, and intertwined the fingers.

It was 9 PM when she woke up and realised she was at his place. A comforter was pulled over her. She went out in the living room. He was watching TV.

"Oh! You are up?! How are you feeling now?"

"I'm better; why did you not wake me up?"

"Go get fresh; I will serve dinner." He ignored her question.

He made soy pulao and tossed some veggies, fried some prawns, and cottage cheese. He was better than her at cooking, she realised. It was 11, and he asked if he could drop her at her place, and she said if it's ok if she stays back.

"You wanna watch a movie?" He asked. She flashed a big smile.

They went to the same room; he turned the lights of the room to a theatrical experience mode, put the AC's temperature just right, popped a big bowl of popcorn, and placed the bean bags in the centre.

"This is so perfect," she said.

"Wait until I play the movie," he whispered in her ears; she got goosebumps.

The movie began with a humongous vessel on the left side of the screen and a crowd waving at it.

"Now it is perfect," he said and fed her popcorn.

The following morning was nothing less than a dream waking up next to each other for them.

"Good morning," they greeted.

"Coffee or tea?" he asked.

"Tea, I'll make it," she replied and headed to the kitchen.

The bell rang; she got alarmed. Who could it be? Ray got the door.

"Hi! Good morning," the person at the door said.

"You're just in time," Ray said.

"How is she now?" the person asked.

Arannya couldn't hold her curiosity and went to check; she was surprised to see Gautam there.

"You guys know each other?" she asked them.

"Yes," they said.

"What!" She was shocked.

"Only since yesterday, we mean," and they laughed.

"Please make a cup for him as well," Ray said and requested Gautam to come in.

While Arannya was sleeping last evening, she was getting continuous calls from Lax, as she was added as an emergency contact for Arannya in her office. It was HR's protocol to inform the concerned person. Ray answered the call and told her she is fine, and she is with him. He shared his location and asked if she could pick her up after a couple of hours since she was sleeping. She said she will try to come; otherwise, send one of her friends. As soon as Gautam learnt about this from Lax, he left his shoot and rushed to Ray's house.

Events of the last evening around 7:30 pm.

Gautam reached his place and called Ray. He answered the call and went down to receive him and told him that she was still sleeping. Ray invited him to his home, but he gracefully refused. He said he will wait for her to wake up and will come back once she is up. Ray asked again if he could come to his place, but he declined his offer again; this time he seemed irked. But since Arannya decided to stay back, the thought of Gautam completely slipped off Ray's mind. At least that's how he reasoned it.

After they finished their tea, Arannya and Gautam left. Ray also got ready, and while he was taking his car out, the guard said, "Gautam is such a strange man Sir." When he asked what made him say that, he told him, Even after Ray requested him to come upstairs, he refused and stayed in his car the entire night! Ray could sense Gautam's feelings towards Arannya; he was happy to know there was someone to look after her, but more than that, he was filled with a certain amount of jealousy. He wanted to be in Gautam's place.

Ray sadly accepted that he and Arannya could only meet in the fields of green.

After lunch, Arannya and Ray went for a short walk around the office premises.

"He's a nice guy, very handsome," he said.

"Who?" She knew who he was referring to.

"Your rescuer, Mr. Gautam." He pulled her leg.

"Yes, that he is, but you were my rescuer if I'm not wrong," she giggled.

Sujith came running towards them and gave them *Paan*. "You guys know that Suman and Devraj have filed for divorce? I overheard some people's conversation at the shop."

"Sujith the reporter! How I wish you were as nosy when it comes to judge collapse in the structures report." Ray mocked as he chewed his betel leaf.

Post-lunch was the most sleepy time of the day but usually a very busy one for everyone in the office. Serendipitously, the servers went down, and this gave a chance for everyone to hit the cafeteria for a nice cup of tea. Whoever knew Arannya and Ray were by now convinced something is brewing between them after Arannya's falling fiasco. They also took it to their advantage but never made things too obvious and played it safe. Since both of them excelled at their work, the higher authorities paid no heed to this. Arannya, Sujith, and Ray sat at the table and ordered tea. Sujith and Ray were discussing how uncomfortable their team is sitting on the designers floor, and they wish to go back to their usual workplace as soon as possible. Arannya took offence, defending that her floor has a much cooler vibe.

"Guys, this Friday we're planning for a potluck!" Sharanya announced.

"Duh! These people and their obsession with Fun Friday. I think they should cook food for the employees too, right? That will add to their repertoire along with making rangolis and blowing balloons. Hahaha." Samar came near their table and passed the statement. Sujith and Ray broke into laughter. Samar sat next to Arannya. But his comment didn't go well with her, and she schooled him about how important HR's role is in an organisation.

"Oh my God! I think you should switch your career to HR. You'll do great!" Sujith mocked her.

"Huh, of course," she affirmed.

"And you are great at making rangoli too, though I'm not sure about the blowing part." Sujith winked at her; she became red with anger and yellow with embarrassment.

"Hahahahaha, that was a good one." Ray commented, and all of them burst out laughing.

"Someone seems to be having a lot of fun here." Dinesh from the finance team came near them; he was accompanied by two more people, including Sharanya.

"Hi Narayan! You look younger these days; what's your sauce?" he said and quickly moved his eyes to Arannya for a second and again back at him.

"Minding your own business, I guess?!" Ray was savage but completely out of character for his docile self. Everyone around could feel the heat.

"So, what are you going to get this Friday? Oh, sorry, wrong question to the wrong person," Dinesh said and continued, "You know, guys, Ray and I have joined this company together, and never in history have I seen him getting home-cooked food."

"Cut the crap, Dinesh! And it's a request not to get the fish fry that you got last time; it really stinks a lot." Sujith cut him short as if he wanted to end the conversation.

"Of course, I will ask my '*wife*' to make pepper chicken this time. What about you, Ray? Oh, apologies again; I know my sister-in-law is quite busy." Dinesh sounded obnoxious; there was a stress on the word wife.

"Not another word!" Sujith became furious, got up from his chair, and Ray held his hand to stop him.

"Take it easy, bro," Dinesh said and left; from there, his company followed him.

Before Arannya could confront Ray, he left right after. She was shaken by the whole thing, and since it involved Ray, she ought to know the story behind this.

"Wanna join me for a smoke?" Sujith was tense.

"Yeah! Let's go, she said and picked up the disposable cups.

They took another cup of tea and sat at the smoking bay. "Motherfucker!" Sujith gnashed his teeth and took a drag.

"Okay! What's going on? Can I know? I'm calling Ray, but he is rejecting my calls."

"I'm not sure if I should be telling you this." Sujith was in a dilemma.

"Don't you think I deserve to know?" She was concerned.

"Actually, you do," he finished his cigarette, rubbed its butt with his shoe, and lit another one.

"Ray's wife and Dinesh belong to the same hometown. When Ray got married, everything was how it was supposed to be. They looked like a perfect couple, went on their honeymoon to Turkey, and within two months she was conceived with Krishaan. That was the time he got a promotion as well. He had quite an enviable life. But things started to change after his wife went to her hometown for the delivery. She gradually reduced the number of calls she would make to Ray. He thought it would be because she was busy looking after herself and never complained since he recently got promoted and couldn't take leaves to be there with her. She was also very supportive. After Krishaan was born, he took a month's leave and went to her hometown; she told him that she'd want to be there until he was old enough to walk and talk. He insisted on coming back with him, but she denied reasoning that she won't be able to manage everything alone, and she has everyone in her home. For three years he used to travel to see the child, and when Krishaan grew up, he again asked her to come along with him. But she seemed reluctant. Since she belonged to a political family, she was richer than him and would turn out to be obnoxious and arrogant at times. One day Krishaan was coming back from playschool, and some goons attacked the car, and the driver was beaten to death. Fortunately, his au pair managed to escape and save his son. It was due to some political rivalry. When Ray got to learn about this, he rushed there, confronted her, told her that his kid was not safe there, and asked her to come with him without further negotiation. She also understood that's the best for them. But even coming to the city, she would feel threatened, told as if someone was following her and Krishaan. Hence they decided to put Krishaan in a boarding school where his maternal aunt would be there to look after him. Even though things were tough, Ray was hopeful that things would start falling into place. She stayed with Ray for 6 months after Krishaan was admitted to boarding, and then she said her mother was not well, and she'd visit her. When even after a month she didn't return, Ray smelt something fishy and asked his friends to snoop on her. They kept an eye on her and got to learn she is having an affair with some person named Rakesh. Further digging into this, they learnt that they were dating before her marriage, but since Rakesh's family was against the union due to class constraints, they got him married to someone else.

After a year she got married to Ray. But during the child's delivery, their lost love ignited again, and old romance rekindled. She fell for him more after learning that he had divorced his wife. When Ray learnt about this, he was shattered. Ray has been a faithful husband. Being the eldest in his family, he never gave in to his desires, never had an affair, and when he got married to her, he knew all his goodness paid off. But "unfair" is another name for life; his life turned upside down; he was now having a cheating wife, and the son he loved was sent afar. He thought of confronting her; on every journey they made to meet Krishaan, he thought of just strangling her and pushing her out of the moving car or crashing the car into a trailer, but the thought of Krishaan losing his mother stopped him. So he suppressed all his emotions and kept it all going with a hope that someday she would come out clean and ask for forgiveness. That never really happened, and he accepted life as is and became docile." Sujith told Arannya.

Arannya was speechless. This was a lot for her to process. "But what's with Dinesh?" she asked.

"Rakesh is Dinesh's elder brother," he answered.

"What!!!" Her jaw dropped.

"Yes, he knew her before he became his wife, and being a douchebag, he told this to many people in the office over a small disagreement with Ray, that motherfucker. Even I was one of the people he told. But I never confronted Ray about this; until one day while he was missing Krishaan very much and asked if I could join him for drinks. That was the time he told me about this."

Arannya was in disbelief.

"You know, after he learnt about his wife's affair, he was broken. He became like a stone; he'd never smile or laugh and would do his work and go home. Even when people commented or asked about his wife's whereabouts, he'd lie and say she's good and never let her dignity be tarnished. Most of the time he turned a deaf ear, but I know how painful it was for him. He became plaintive; his pride was shattered, and he accepted the way life turned out for him. But when you came to this office, I had seen him taking interest in someone for the first time, like when it was your first day and you seemed lost; it was him who asked me to come and speak to you. Even in the cafeteria it was him who asked me to call you to sit with us. It was after a long time I saw him smiling, and that gave relief to my heart. He is like a big brother to me. He has helped me every time I was in any kind of trouble, be it financial or getting beaten by police over a road rage. I count on him blindly, and I would give up my life for him if need be. That is why I always encourage you guys and get so happy to see you two together. Trust me, he cares for you more than he shows. He deserves true love, and I could see that potential in you, Aaru."

Arannya was in tears, her throat choked with emotions. How can he be handling so much in his life, so much pain, with so much grace? She fell in love with him harder. Instead of hating his wife, she was feeling pitiful towards her; how could she have the best man in the world and still cheat? She felt like running towards him and hugging him and telling him that she'd be there for him no matter what. He saw her before she knew him and was genuinely concerned about her. He knew she needed someone, and he made sure he was there, directly or indirectly. How could he be such a good Samaritan and keep himself under wraps? She called him, but his phone was turned off; she went to the office and saw he had left for the day.

She went straight to his place but couldn't find him there; after a while, she received a text from him: "I had to leave early; don't worry; I'll be back by Monday. Take care."

Where he went, she had no clue; all she could do was wait patiently. She was reminded of the time when Karan left her for weeks in a similar fashion. She came back home and told Lax everything; she cursed his wife and told Arannya if she wants, she can be with him; that's the right thing to do, since his wife is already enjoying her life, why would these guys not do the same?

"It's not that simple, Lax."

"Oh! Hell, it's that simple, Akka." Lax said.

Arannya's phone rang; she took it out in a hurry from her bag, hoping it was him, but it was a call from Gwen.

"Is that him?" Lax asked.

"No, this is Gwen, my old friend." She shook her head and answered the call.

"Hey, hi, Gwen, tell me? I'm doing well; how are you? That's such great news; congratulations! Give my love to the baby boy." Arannya said over the call.

"Yeah, all good; life's passing by. Oh! Please drop the subject already; I'm in fact deciding on never getting hitched; I will adopt your baby boy. Hahaha." After listening to Gwen for some 10 minutes, she said, "No!

What kind of question is that? I have nothing to do with him now. Yeah, let it be on his head. I have no business with him. Make it clear to him. Okay, you take care; we'll talk later. Bye." Arannya said and hung up. Lax was curious to know what the conversation was about.

She told him it was nothing and told her she'd need some rest and went inside her room.

Arannya took a cold shower; she had a lot to process. She was wondering that a few days ago, Karan's thoughts crept in, and today Gwen called and said that Karan has filed for a divorce, and he told Gwen how sorry he was and wanted to reconcile things with Arannya. Gwen asked if she could give another chance. She thought on this, because she was really in love with Karan back then, and if only Ray wouldn't have happened to her life, she might have given it a thought, but she's already named her heart for Ray. Karan stands no chance.

That week went like a punishment for her. Going to the office and seeing his empty chair made her feel miserable. She was dejected but had to put on a brave face and reminisce in their good memories to keep up with this predicament. Loss of appetite made her shed some fat. She went on a liquid diet and refrained from any kind of enjoyment. She wanted to get consumed by his feelings. As if she's painted in his love, and when she enjoyed the pleasures, she had to respect and endure the pain too.

Next Monday, he showed up in the office. She was elated to see him but upset over the thought that he did not call her until then. She went near him and greeted, "Good morning." He was so immersed in the computer screen that he did not look at her and responded with an onomatopoeic Hmm. She was taken aback. During lunch break, she asked him if everything was okay. He said it was. While eating he'd always give the sweet from his plate to her, but that day he forgot that. This was a very small thing, but she noticed it. After they finished, usually Sujith, Arannya, and Ray would take a stroll, but he said he had some important work to attend to and went back.

"What's with him?" Arannya asked Sujith.

"Nothing, You're over analysing now. Let's go grab some smoke." Sujith said.

At the time of leaving, they'd wait for each other to finish their tasks, but he came to her desk and said he was leaving for the day.

"Okay, wait for me; I'm almost done," she said.

"Actually, I have to meet my cousin now. You drive safe, okay? See you tomorrow."

"I need to talk," she said.

"Can it wait till tomorrow?" he asked.

"Sure," she said, her throat was filled with undropped tears; she could clearly see him distancing himself from her, but why is he doing that? She couldn't understand. She was trying hard not to break down and struggled to gulp her tears. She could sense something in him had changed. The reason was a mystery. She was going crazy over this altercation. But thinking about his life, she felt sorry for him and in no way wanted to be an add-on trouble. She just rolled over and played dead to the entire debacle. When she asked the next day if they could grab beer and he refused, she took it sportily. When he refused to join for lunch, citing he had some work to finish, she made herself understand that it's nothing, and he must really be occupied. But her patience was waning. However, the fight that she was giving to come out as the displeasure caused by the paradigm shift in the dynamics between them made her completely non compos mentis.

She decided to change the course of things and trade thoughtfully with him. While Ray had faced the truth that his actions were giving her momentary happiness but would shatter her in the long run, he started distancing himself. And Arannya was just blind to everything; all she wanted was to make things go back to how they were when they were love-struck.

What would she gain out of it? Nonchalant and befuddled, she lost touch with reality; sooner or later, this had to end. Relationships like this are often destined to meet the fate of a mayfly. They are short-lived but full of life. One can live an entire life in it, or one can live an entire life and still be unknown to its contentment. Only a lucky few ill-fated souls who have experienced this can understand the magic it possesses and the pleasure it yields. It gives the experience of a lifetime with every emotion stripped naked, enabling a person to see who they really are; it gives them the power to unleash their darkest desires and fathom themselves at the soul level.

Will she fall in the fifth category? Will she have it all?

It was a Thursday, and the following Friday was a holiday due to some festival. She knew this was her chance, so she booked two tickets for a movie and texted him, "Tomorrow 12 pm, PVR." He reacted to her text with a thumbs up. A sign of positivity after so long mellowed her out.

She took the cab to the theatre; she had planned the whole day. First they'll watch the movie, then she'll take him window shopping, and after that they'll go bowling, and for dinner she booked his favourite fine-dining restaurant. She was assured that since she'd not gotten her car, he would offer to either drive her to her place or take her to his. Secretly, she hoped for it to be the latter.

She wore a blue denim mini skirt and a white Bardot top, knee-length suede boots, and a bubblegum pink trench coat. She wanted to look appealing and show him she can rock the western look as well. One of the reasons she loved winters was she could style herself like a European. She ditched her usual specs, wore an animal print frame, and completed her look with a white crossbody hobo bag. She was feeling confident in her skin. She reached the mall and was waiting on the ground floor for him to come. She was strolling around in a watch showroom; it's been 5 minutes; he should be here in another 5, she thought. It's 10 minutes, and he hasn't called her yet. Lately, as the situation between them suddenly went off-tune, she refrained from calling him and checking if he'd come. In fact, she was afraid to call him and hear a rejection. Hence, she decided to dress up and go to the mall directly, with a positive mindset. She came out of the showroom; 15 minutes remained for the movie, and now she became sceptical whether or not he'll show up. She was strolling aimlessly when her phone rang. It was him!

"Hi," he greeted.

"Hey," she was excited.

"Where are you?" he asked.

"What do you mean? In the mall, where else? We have a movie, right?" She sensed something wasn't right.

"Yeah, I know, but due to some exigent circumstances, I couldn't make it. I'm so sorry." He apologised.

She was filled with angst and disappointment; tears started to roll down her cheeks instantly.

"Hello, Aarna, are you there?" he asked. She chose not to respond. She became silent. She wiped her tears and pulled herself together.

"Hello, hello, Aarna?" he asked again.

"Yes, I'm here. No problem, take care," she said and hung up. She could hear he was still saying something, but she didn't wish to listen to him at this point in time. She was left disheartened. But there wasn't really anything that she could do about the reverse state of affairs. She thought she had done everything in her life alone: travelled alone, shopped alone, attended hospital check-ups alone, went to the restaurant alone, but never a movie. 'Well, there's always a first time.' She pep talked to herself and decided to go and watch the movie alone. After she hung up, he was calling her continuously, but she ignored it. She was very angry at him. In any case, what could she do? She was not his girlfriend; was she even a friend? What was she even? These questions made her go nuts. Regardless, she took the escalators to reach the multiplex. As she reached the multiplex entrance, her phone was buzzing continually. Annoyed, she put it on aeroplane mode. She scanned the ticket and went inside.

And saw him there.

He was looking at her and giggling. She was fuming with anger; her tears started to roll again. He walked up to her and asked, "Popcorn or nachos or both?"

"Get some coke mixed with poison." She snapped at him.

He ordered a combo and asked the server to get it at their seats.

"Let's go?" he said and held her hand. Making all her anger vanish instantaneously.

Throughout the movie They didn't leave their hands. She fed him the snacks, and he held the cold drink cup. They watched the entire movie without talking to each other.

Arannya was having lots of questions in her mind, but she waited for the right moment. It was the ending scene of the movie; she leaned on his hand, and he rested his head on hers. The lights turned on, and they corrected their position.

Even though he was next to her, she felt the emotional discord. She could feel his presence was fragmentary. She asked him if things were alright and only got a yes in response.

"That was a nice movie," he said while they came out of the theatre.

"Yeah," she agreed.

He went and stood in front of the elevator.

"Where are you going? We have to go to the floor below," she said.

"What for?" he asked.

"Surprise," she whispered and took him to a bowling arcade. He had once told her that no one can beat him at bowling, so she challenged him.

"Why do you want to cry again?" he chuckled.

"We'll see," she smirked.

They ordered beer and cheese balls and started the game.

Ray was right; he was really a pro at bowling. He achieved a bagger. Arannya, who thought she would win, was struggling with the hard spares. But seeing how enthusiastic he was while playing it and the smile he flashed after hitting each strike made it worth the tears for her. There were only three more rounds left. Arannya thought she'd lost the game anyway. Let's do it with a decent score at least. She took a heavier ball this time; with full vigour, she ran towards the lane only to crown an embarrassing slip.

"Ouch!" She whined in pain.

Ray ran towards her and slipped too. They both looked at each other and laughed hysterically. Thankfully it wasn't a serious fall.

"You alright!?" he asked.

"Couldn't be better," she answered as she looked at him smiling and laughing.

"Enough of this; let me drop you home now." He said as he helped her get up.

"What? No, we have to finish the beer, and after that I planned to go shopping, which I think we'll have to drop and directly go for dinner." she said.

"Look at you!! No shopping, no dinner. I will drop you home now," he announced.

After he finished his beer, they took the elevator and went to the basement. Arannya was determined to have a tough conversation with him and call a spade a spade. She thought he'd take her to his place, but to her disappointment, he was dropping her at hers. She understood that he came to the movie just to keep her heart, but he clearly seemed uninterested. As soon as they got in the car, she asked,

"What is wrong with you?"

"What do you mean?"

"I need to know; I could feel the change towards me."

"Why do you think that? I am just the same."

"Oh! Are you? Don't let me open my mouth now." Arannya was angry.

"Go on, I'm listening." He remained calm.

"For some days you are maintaining a distance from me, ignoring me. Even if you don't say it, I could just feel it. Today as well I thought you'd call me before the movie and pick me up, but you did not. In the movie as well, I thought you'd caress my hair and kiss me on my hand, but you didn't. You did not even hug me till now!" she complained.

"And what made you think I'd do that?" His tone changed.

Listening to this Arannyas mind blew away. Is that really him talking?

"What do you mean, Ray? You know what I feel towards you, and you too feel for me." She was not in her senses; otherwise, she'd have never said that being sober.

"No! I don't know what you're talking about! I consider you as my good friend, in fact one of the closest, but I think I have given you the wrong impression. I talk to you and am with you because I like you as a person; that doesn't mean I am into you or something," he said, and continued, "I thought you were a mature girl and would take things in good taste, but no, you are still a teenager. It was all platonic." He said and started the car.

"Platonic!?" She repeated the word in bewilderment and started to cry; she couldn't believe her ears. This is not how he speaks; this is someone else. She doesn't recognise this person.

"Put on the seat belt," he said. She was sitting lifeless and did not respond; he took the belt and buckled up.

"You are kidding, right?" she sobbed nonstop.

"Arannya, I am really sorry if because of me you are feeling this way. But don't you know I have a family? Have I ever lied about it or hidden anything from you?"

She thought of telling him that she knows his marriage is a sham, but she held back. What had gotten into him suddenly? Everything was hunky-dory, then what happened now? She knew he was happy with her, loved her; she had felt the love for her in his eyes, in his care. Though he never expressed it verbally, the little things he did weren't a white lie.

"So. You mean all the time we spent together, those moments on the trip, were zilch?" she asked.

"That's not what I meant, Arannya, but if that would make you understand things, then yes, it was nothing. Happy!" He said as he approached her place.

'What were you thinking, Aaru? What were you thinking? How could you get yourself into this? How can you think this could have a future? Wake up, Aarna.' She whispered to herself as she sobbed perpetually. To her surprise, Ray remained unmoved and maintained a stoic demeanour. He did not even ask what she was murmuring. Did not even wipe her tears or pass her tissues.

"Please pull over," she snivelled.

"I'm dropping you at your place." He was determined.

"Pull over, I said". She was loud; this time her wrath could be felt.

He stopped the car sideways; the road was less busy as the area quartered government employees. The square was a km away from there. She unbuckled herself.

"Where are you going?" he was concerned.

"Don't worry; I know I'm stupid, but not to an extent to sabotage myself!" She got down.

"Aarna, please," he pleaded.

"It's Arannya, Mr. Narayan!" She tried hard to stop her tears, but one stubborn droplet fell from her right eye, and she walked away.

Ray knew she would not stop for anything. She is gone. He wanted this to happen.

He stayed in the car, numb and speechless like an immovable object, and tears started to roll down. He banged his head on the steering wheel and cried like a heartbroken teenager. After all, this was the first time he faced a heartbreak, for what his wife did to him was no less than a sin. The pain of losing his love was unbearable for him. He knew he lost her. He felt terrible about himself. But this was best for her because if he did not step back, she could never think about her future. This is going to hurt her, but eventually she'll come to terms with it. She will be okay; she has her whole life ahead of her, and he has lived his life. How can he be so selfish? He cursed himself. He felt so low about himself that he wanted to commit hara-kiri. He loved her truly, more than anything in the world. He loved her truly; hence, he let her go.

On the other hand, she loved him unconditionally and was ready to remain single forever and be by his side. But he did not want her to disregard her life for him and wanted only the best. He thought for a moment about divorcing his wife, and when Krishaan would grow up, he would understand his father, but what about Arannya? People, his family, and the society will charge her maliciously, calling her names, homewrecker and other unimaginable hurtful things, which he never wanted her to go through. He could listen to all this, but he would kill if anyone said that to her. And how many of them could he really kill? Being together meant nothing less than a bloodbath. He had to put an end to this; doing this calmly wouldn't have helped the storm that she was.

Only a hurricane could tame a storm.

She was his first love, and he, her last.

Arannya unconsciously kept walking till she reached her place. She changed her clothes, took her bag, and went straight to the airport.

'I'm going home for a few days; everything is fine. Take care.' She left a message for Lax and posted it on the refrigerator. She knew if she called her now she'd get worried and rush home. She switched her phone off.

This phase was the twilight of her life, and, in a literal sense, she wore tinted glasses to hide her tears and took the next flight home.

It was two hours after midnight when she reached her home. She has not informed her parents; her mom was taken by surprise to see her at the door, that too without any luggage.

"Oh my God, Aaru, what happened? Is everything alright? Why haven't you informed us? We would have sent someone to pick you up!" Her mom opened the door as she used to study late at night.

"Yes, all good. I was missing home, so here I am." She said,

"You did the right thing; just inform us next time," her mom said and took her in.

"Should I wake your father?"

"No, Mom, I will meet him in the morning."

"Should I serve you something to eat?" her mom asked another question.

"Oh God, no, Maa, you continue with your things; I am too tired and need some rest. Don't wake me up early. Good night." She sounded cranky, but it's only with her mom that she could behave like a spoiled brat.

Everything in her room was kept as is. The smell of her room and the comfort of her bed gave her the sleep she needed. Her mind was flooded with thoughts that it was congested. It was so worn out that she went to sleep instantaneously.

She did not touch her phone for the next two days. Lax and Gautam were worried, but Lax knew one thing about her: she wouldn't harm herself. Being the only child to her parents keeps reminding her of her responsibility towards them. She told her parents that she needed a break and impulsively flew home. Though her parents knew there was more to it, they gave her time to settle and waited for her to share. She had a peaceful time with her digital detox. The only positive thing her failed relations did was to teach her the coping mechanisms and how to be bigger than the circumstances.

For the last two days, she read magazines, read newspapers with Papa at the swing, helped the gardener with watering the plants, took over the cook's job in the kitchen, took walks around her city, and saw a fair. She felt like a child again; she called Shiney to check if she was in town, but she wasn't.

She wanted to walk down her childhood, so she asked her mom to give her keys to the attic and went through her dadu's books and belongings, her toys, and her favourite comic books. When she saw "Idgah," she became nostalgic and sobbed. That was the last story she recited to her Dadu.

"Then darling, you become that person," Dadus' words echoed in her ears. She held the book close to her heart and cried her heart out.

"I did, Dadu. I always become 'that' person to keep someone else's needs above mine and love them, but nobody wanted that," and she had a good cry; her heart felt lighter. As she was going through other items, like the greeting cards she received from Kartik, it made her cry again. 'I miss you, Kartik. If only you were alive, I would be saved from this living hell,' she cried more. 'I hope you are happy wherever you are because living in this world is a punishment, not some blessing. I wish I had been riding with you that day.' She cried some more.

Then she went through Shiney and her artworks and her songbook, in which she used to write lyrics of the songs; her eyes fell on a tin cookie box; as she opened it, she saw the sketch pen set that Sajan lent her. 'You are the real culprit! If you could have told me directly to meet you, we would have ended up together, and I would have been saved from all that happened in my life!' In angst she tore the sketch pen packet and saw there was something written on the backside of the brand paper: *'I love you, Arannya. Meet me at 4 at Bunny Bun if you do too! I'll be waiting!'*

"Oh, Mi Vida Loca!" She pulled her hair and lay flat on the floor and cried and laughed and laughed and cried!

On Monday she turned her phone on, and as expected, her inbox was filled with messages, and there was a long trail of missed calls. Somewhere she felt happy that at least he cares, but her little happiness was short-lived and swiftly turned into disappointment as she saw they were all from either Lax or Gautam. She did not receive a single text or a call from Ray! That was it for them. Her heart died a little. How could he turn so rancorous? She couldn't believe his capricious behaviour, but she had to believe her jinxed fate.

For the rest of the week, her mom and dad showed her profiles after profiles of suitors, 5 at breakfast, 10 at lunch, and 20 at dinner. She kept on turning them down for bizarre reasons, like one is way too handsome for her, and all her life would pass in insecurity! They gave up on their mission. But when she was about to leave for her work town, they resorted to that one weapon, which was a Brahmastra for every parent out there. "Melodramatic emotional intimidation." Her mom told her that they have never forced her into anything; she wanted to pursue anything but law, and they agreed to it even after building a whole fortune for her out of it. They never put pressure on her to carry their legacy, but they only have one wish: to see their daughter get settled. They are not even forcing her to marry someone of their choice but whoever she wants; alas, even that seemed like a far-fetched dream for Arannya.

In Indian society, getting settled has nothing to do with your established career or impressive bank balance, but being married. Even if only the couple would know what's under the facade, they'll be known as settled in their life. This mentality has kept so many people from being happy.

Listening to her ageing parents made her think over her decision to not get married. Can she do that? Just to keep them happy? Should she find someone like her who has also lost interest and doesn't want to get married but has to due to family pressure? Not a bad idea, she thought.

If only life was as easy as we thought; from where else would we get all the adrenaline rush from?

She knew a part of her heart died. Oozing blood whenever she remembered Ray, the red room slowly began to turn to stone. The aura she carried was so sad that anyone passing her by could feel it. She was allotted a window seat, which could allow her to weep privately under her eye masks. A couple sat next to her with a small baby. From their conversation and excitement, she figured they were flying for the first time. They asked the air hostess if they could get the window seat. The hostess declined politely. Arannya offered them her window seat. They looked elated. Which made Arannya smile. The air hostess saw what she did and complimented her with an appreciation card saying,

'People like you make the world beautiful! Keep spreading the love :)' - Deepanshi.

Arannya, who was feeling hopeless and worthless about her life and herself, suddenly was filled with gratitude. This simple act of kindness came back to her when she needed it the most and lifted her spirits. Instant Karma, they say.

She dropped a message to Lax and asked if she could come to pick her up. It was 6:30 in the evening when she landed; she got a message from Lax that she's at pick-up zone 3.

"Akka! I missed you." Lax said as she started the car.

"I know, missed you too," Arannya reciprocated.

"How is Uncle Aunty? And what did you get for me?"

"They are doing fine, and sorry I couldn't get anything for you."

"There's no easy slide with this one!" Lax stated.

"Yes, I owe you one! And how are things at work?" Arannya asked.

"Same Akka, but these newcomers are a real pain in the arse, I swear! They should stick to two-minute reels of social media; being working behind a big screen is way too different, and above that they think so little of us!" Lax complained.

"Hmm," she responded.

Lax knew she wasn't looking well and refrained from talking. Arannya pretended to sleep.

After they reached their place, Lax made a call to someone.

"You guys ready?" She asked.

"Yes, we are!" They said,

When Lax opened the door, it was all dark; as soon as Arannya turned the lights on, she was taken by surprise! Chaitra, Emraan, Daniel, Rishi, and Gautam shouted, "Happy Birthday!" They decorated the entire hall with red balloons. And a huge 12-inch Belgian chocolate cake was placed at the centre table. "Happy birthday, A," it read.

It was her birthday. Ever since her 10th std, she has refrained from celebrating her birthday as it reminded her of the irreversible loss.

Gautam stepped forward; he was looking his best that day. He came straight from his shoot wearing his character's costume. White shirt, folded sleeves, and suspenders. Arannya was spellbound. What exactly is stopping her from embracing this man's love? She's been rough on her heart. Can she also have a normal life? But what if Gautam hurts her too? These thoughts popped into her mind.

Garuav took her bag, held her hand, and said, "Let's not keep the cake waiting!"

"Thank you very much, guys, but I am sorry I don't celebrate my birthday." She said and left his hand.

"A person who dwells in the past can never make memories." Gautam stated.

"We're aware of the reason, Aaru, but can you break your rule for us?" Chaitra said. The atmosphere became a little heavy, as Arannya did not say a word.

"Ok, we've got a solution to that! Mr. Gautam, please cut the cake on behalf of 'Your Mehboob.'" Emraan teased him and attempted to lighten the mood.

"Let's skip the cutting and just dig our glasses into it!" Chaitra said and got the wine glasses.

"Guys, we only got six glasses; someone needs to share." Chaitra requested.

"Gautam and Arannya will share, of course." This was Rishi with contemptuous body language.

After they ate the cake, Lax said she'd take her leave as she had a special episode shoot scheduled. And others also left soon since it was a working day tomorrow.

In the end, only Gautam was left. He picked up the glasses and kept them in the sink. Arannya knew he was disappointed because of her sudden disappearance. She waited for him to speak, but he didn't say anything.

Gautam was holding himself back since it was her birthday. He just wanted to do something so special that the past wound will be washed off and she gets a reason to celebrate her birthday hereon. But his efforts didn't seem to come to fruition.

Arannya was sitting quietly and watching him do the things.

"Okay then, happy birthday once again. I'll take my leave now." He said and searched for his wallet in his pocket.

"Thank you," she said as she stared at him.

He couldn't find his wallet and was searching around when she said, "If you are not having your shoot, accompany me for a glass of wine."

He was searching behind the pillows on the sofa and stopped when she said that. He turned to her and asked in a quirky way, "Here or on the balcony?" and went to the kitchen to clean and get the glasses. He was thrilled but was successful in hiding that.

"Balcony," she smiled.

They came outside; some of the balloons flew from the hall and settled in the balcony, beautifying the ambience. The cold breeze of the moonless night and fog just of the right amount made it look perfect.

He asked her to be seated, and he went inside Lax's room to get a warm shawl and draped it over her. He was looking out for something.

"What are you searching for?" she asked.

"Where are the wood logs?" he questioned.

"In the storeroom, I guess. Are you making a bonfire?" she asked.

"You're a smart one, aren't you!" He said sarcastically. "Growing wiser and younger," he winked.

She was observing him as he arranged the bonfire pit. The wood seemed to have moistened, so he poured some whisky and lit it up.

"Perfecto!" He exclaimed and blew a chef's kiss.

"Let's open the wine now." He said, Arannya got a call as he was pouring the wine; it was from Shiney. She's always been the last person to call her, albeit being her best friend! He raised one eyebrow, indicating to her to keep the phone aside. She got the cue and put it on silent.

"Thank you, Gautam!" She was filled with gratitude.

"Hmm," he responded.

"And I'm sorry too. I wasn't in my right mind, so I had to leave like that," she explained.

"We'll keep that for later. For now let's honour this wine," he responded.

"Yeah!" she said. She was feeling much lighter, and Gautam was such a person who could make any awkward situation likeable.

"Can I ask you something?" asked Arannya.

"Go on," he nodded.

She sipped the wine and asked, "Why are you so good to me?"

"Oh my God, if you still don't get it, then I think I am doing something wrong in my life! Haven't I made it obvious on occasion after occasion, time and again, what I feel for you, Aaru?"

"You did…"

"Then?"

"Gautam, you are a great person! Well-mannered and a handsome-looking man. Any girl would want to be with you."

"Then, why can't it be you?" He questioned.

"Because…" she paused.

"Because?" he repeated.

"Because I cannot love anyone. I have lost that artistry. And I cannot do injustice to someone knowing he deserves love, which I cannot provide," she said and continued, "Gautam, I don't have a very impressive history when it comes to matters of the heart. And I don't have much hope in this regard either. I have always gotten what I wished for; being a single child, I never had to struggle for anything, but this area is certainly doomed. Trust me. Trust me, I have tried earlier, but I was faced with deceit and defeat each time. Therefore, I don't want to put my heart through this all over again. The impact of living in the world of fairy tales and fantasies in my childhood was so deep that I started to believe I'd also marry the one I love. But life is no fantasy. Having no burden of expectations and being born with a silver spoon made me turn into an absolute egotist. I am so engrossed in myself that I completely overlooked the fact that my parents are ageing, and they have only one expectation from me: to get settled. Hence, I have made up my mind! I will get married now. But I will only marry someone who doesn't believe in this institution and wants to get married just for the sake of it. This way I will be honest with him and free from the burden of loving someone," she said and took a deep breath. Gautam was looking in her eyes without blinking.

What happened next left her speechless.

"Marry me," he said.

"What!? This is not a joke!" She exclaimed.

"This is not a joke." He said and took a platinum band from his pinky finger, went on his knees, and proposed to her.

This was totally unexpected for her. She knew he liked her, but marriage is a big thing.

As he couldn't balance any longer, he got up and kept the ring in her hand. She kept the palm open and gazed at it. The faraway gaze in her eyes caught his attention. He closed her palm and said, "You don't have to answer me right away. Take your time and think it over from all the perspectives; forget about whether you are able to give me love or not. My prerequisite is you should allow yourself to be loved. You should allow me to love you. That's all."

"But, Gautam...."

"Shhhh ... . Don't say anything; if you feel that I am capable enough to love you, just wear that, and I'll know. Otherwise keep it as your birthday present." He cut her short, kissed her forehead, and left.

She was flabbergasted.

'I need to see my therapist.' She whispered to herself.

Arannya was overwhelmed by how the events unfolded and had no idea how to navigate her way out of it. Looking from another's point of view, she was just one decision away from having it all figured out. However, the water often seems calm on the surface; only the ocean knows the turbulence within. Her heart was still bleeding, and the only thing that could stop it was Ray himself. She does acknowledge the fact that Gautam is the perfect man for her.

But the yearning of the heart surpasses all logic, for argumentation is not its forte. It is aloof from the otherworldly characteristics and is only familiar to how it feels around the one made for him. And Arannya's heart knew that it desired only Ray, not anyone else.

They were soulmates after all.

Contemplating the ring for some odd hours, she nodded off. The next day she overslept; her alarm did its best to wake her up after every ten minutes but lost to her dreamy sleep.

She has thought over the situationship with Ray. She decided to put in her papers and cut her heart some slack. She was determined to ignore him completely as if he never existed. In spite of all the resolutions, she wore the kurti that he bought her and his favourite perfume.

She saw his car and parked hers right next to his. She secretly wished for him to see her and melt down. With all the determination to ignore him, she went on her floor only to be disappointed to see someone else sitting in his place. After a little interrogation, she learnt that even though the upper floor's renovation was incomplete, the QC team demanded to be moved to their original places, as this floor was too noisy. They requested the team to get the workers on task during the non-office hours. This situation should have made her feel better; this is what she wanted at the end of the day. But it left her anxious and breathless instead.

She wanted to show him she's doing just fine without him, but the universe deprived her of that pleasure even.

At lunch, she decided to sit alone like in earlier days. But she knew if Sujith saw her, he'd definitely call her, and he did too. She said she'd sit alone, but as expected, he insisted. She thought, this is her moment to ignore Ray. But deep in her heart she was dying to see him.

After a couple of minutes he entered the cafeteria and walked past her and ignored her as if she weren't there.

He has started to eat lunch with the managerial panel since last week. She couldn't eat her lunch; the ignorance from Ray was worse than death for her. Sujith pretended as if nothing happened and was talking about random things. She thought Sujith would talk about Ray and tell her why he is not eating with them; nonetheless, he didn't.

"Aarna, eat your food!" Sujith noticed she wasn't eating anything.

"Hmm, yeah," she said and ate some curd.

A few moments later, Sharanya came to her and asked, "Hey, you were on leave last week; hope everything's fine."

"Yeah, all good. I just visited my parents," Arannya answered.

"Oh, I see. By the way, what happened to Ray? He's not eating with you guys?" Sharanya asked in an attempt to irk her and left from there, hitting the spot.

Arannya looked at Sujith for answers; he refrained from speaking. She hardly ate anything and reasoned that she'd had a heavy breakfast, but Sujith knew the reason. After some time she saw Ray walking towards them. Her heart raced, hoping he would notice what she wore and acknowledge her presence.

"Get the reports ready and set the call." He came and instructed Sujith but did not even look at her. Not even a passing glance. As if she was invisible.

Sujith saw her eyes; she was about to cry. Unable to put her act together, she kept the plate and rushed to the restroom. The one near the cafeteria was usually less occupied. She turned all the taps on and cried, fuming with anger and the humiliation she suffered; she slapped herself hard. No one was to be blamed for her miserable state of affairs but herself. Her cheeks swelled as the fingers got imprinted on them.

'He was never mine, so why is this hurting me so much? When I was determined to not get hurt and just keep loving him, then why had these expectations taken over me?' She spoke to herself. Maybe because even if he couldn't love her back, he stripped off her rights to love him either. This hurt her the most.

All she wanted was to love him selflessly, but is there anything as such?

She washed her face and went to her desk.

"What happened to your face?" Vrushab, who sits next to her, asked.

"I don't know, some reaction maybe," she answered and hit the spacebar on her keyboard.

Trying hard not to cry, she focused on her work. All the memories with Ray, which were mostly only the happy ones, started to play in her mind. The fact that she'll never get to live them again killed her. It was as if she wanted a toy, and she got it for some time but was snatched away abruptly by someone who owned it. Sujith came to her floor after two hours and took her for a coffee break.

"I expected you earlier!" she complained.

"Yeah, I know. I'm sorry. You wait near the entrance; I'll get my car."

"Why a car? Where are we going?"

"To drink a nice cup of mocha java," he said and headed to the basement.

It was a 10-minute drive, and they reached a cafe, which was newly inaugurated. "You pick a place to sit; I'll order and come." Sujith said.

Arannya looked around at the empty seats in the garden and sat at the one in the middle near the big banyan tree.

Sujith came and placed the receipt and keys on the table.

"Tell me what's going on." Arannya asked.

"Promise me you won't do anything stupid!" He asked her to pledge.

She's heard those lines before. Who has said this in the past? She was trying hard to remember.

"Aaru? Promise me." he repeated.

"Of course I promise, please, now tell me? Why is he not eating with us? Is it because of me?"

"The thing is, his wife is back," he informed her.

She was taken aback, like this was the last nail in the coffin for her feelings towards Ray. She did not want to hear what he said; she wished this was a lie and Ray would come there to make it up with her.

"Also, Ray has put his papers in." Sujith said.

"What? When? How could he! Let me call him!" She was disoriented by this news.

"Arannya, wait. Hear me out first." Sujith stopped her from dialling Ray.

"I don't know what happened between you two, but Ray called me last Sunday, and he was crying like a baby. Now imagine a person who hardly smiles how difficult it'd have been for him to cry in front of another person. I was taken aback. He said he has messed up and doesn't know what to do. I requested that he come to my place. He told you guys had a spat and he was upset about it; the same night he got a call from his wife, and she was crying regretfully. His wife finally came clean and asked for his forgiveness. She sounded genuinely sorry for what she did to him and even agreed to a divorce if he wishes to leave her. But he did not say a word; all he could think about was his son. When he kept silent, she thought there was still a chance for them and wished to come back home to make things right. He was stuck in a whirlwind of emotions. After thinking thoroughly, he decided to forgive his wife. This was the best for everyone, Ray said." Sujith told Arannya.

Arannya was dumbfounded.

"Best for everyone, yeah?! Who is this everyone? He, his wife, and his son! Yes, perfect, good for them. God bless them!" Her voice was shaking, and tears started to roll out.

"He said staying in the same office would make things awkward and difficult for you; hence he decided to put his papers in." Sujith added.

"Awesome!" she wiped her perpetually flowing tears.

The hot java turned cold.

"Let's go." She got up and aggressively took a bunch of tissue papers from the box.

"Arannya," Sujith wanted to tell her something else.

"What?" She blew her nose on the tissue to clear the snot while the tears kept flowing.

"He is moving to the states in three months."

She couldn't hold it any longer and bawled like a person who's lost a near one.

"I am so sorry, Aaru. I am so sorry." He hugged her and let her cry. Her plight even made Sujith shed a tear.

"Please don't take me back to the office," she sobbed.

"Sure," he said, and they drove off.

She came home late that night, was so drunk as if the alcohol would flush out her emotions. Sujith, who was sober, dropped her off at her place; Lax took her in, and she went straight to her room. This felt like the end of her life. She was suicidal. Until now it was just Ray, and she knew that even though he was married and had a child, he was staying alone. But now things have changed; his "*wife*" is back. Which means he'd go back to *her* at the end of the long, tiring day and not to her for a pint of beer. He'd talk about his day to *her*, cook dinner for *her*, watch movies with *her*, feed *her* popcorn, and sleep with *her*! She couldn't think further; in rage, she dug her nails so hard on her knees that the blood showed up, but this pain was nothing compared to her mournful heart.

"Love is not for the ordinary," she heard the autophony.

The office, which was once her Disneyland, now became a graveyard of her dead hopes with dried flowers of broken emotions. The dramatic change in Ray towards Arannya left her traumatised. She was appalled by his ignorance, but he behaved indifferently. He unapologetically gave her a cold shoulder. And made it sure to avoid her in every possible way. He changed his car parking space and made sure to keep it between two already parked cars. Already started to eat with the other team and maintained distance even from Sujith, he walked past her like a complete stranger.

She'd lost all her faith in the superpower, and given up all hopes; for the kind of luck she bore, had nothing to do with love. Day after day he kept ignoring her. She dreaded going to the office, but even after losing all the hope, she still vouched for a miracle.

Because only a divine intervention could bring them together now.

Life, however unfair, for once, miraculously turns out to be in one's favour and gives one the moment to change their destiny forever.

And they were the ill-fated chosen ones!

Arannya's predicament pushed her to the depths of depression. Her frequent mood changes, numbness, and anxiety made her aloof in the office. She could not concentrate on her work. There was an escalation about her absentmindedness. She was advised to take a sabbatical. But she refused. How could she? She knew he would be leaving in three months. After that she had no way to see him even. She knew how it is to not be able to see or talk to someone you love; Kartik's loss has taught her enough.

Having a pessimistic approach towards the outer circumstances, she was still a hopeless optimist from within. Even in this situation she was thankful to be able to see Ray. And she did not want to lose it or miss any chance to see him; she was just clutching at straws.

It was a weekend, and Arannya wanted to be locked in her room and sleep. Lax saw this and asked Gautam what's the matter. He said he was unaware of this, as he was swamped for a few weeks and couldn't really check on her. But he deliberately kept a distance and waited for Arannya to reply to his proposal, and he avoided calling or meeting her out of the fear of rejection, so he wanted to give her as much time and space as possible and went missing in action with Arannya.

Lax was worried about Arannya's state and did something she knew wouldn't go down well with her, but unable to see her condition, she did it anyway and dialled Ray. They spoke for nearly an hour, where Lax was blaming him that he was responsible for Arannya's situation. She asked Ray if Akka had demanded anything out of him. He said no.

Then why is he making her life a living hell? She accused him. Ray, to her surprise, did not retaliate but heard her out completely. Then he asked if he could say something; Lax had no interest in listening to him; all she wanted was for him to not treat Arannya like this. 'Yeah, go ahead,' she said. And after listening to Ray, Lax had a total change of perspective towards him. She was in tears knowing how helpless he was. He asked her to do him a favour; even after knowing this was going to give Arannya a near-death experience, she agreed to it. How could life be so unfair towards two people who truly love each other? Lax wondered. She was in tears.

The next day she went to Arannya's room for breakfast. Arannya said she didn't feel like having it.

"You think I am going to give up so easily, Akka?" Laxmi asked.

"Why do you do this, Lax?" She said and got up.

"Lax the invincible!" Lax said and winked. "Finish the breakfast quickly and get ready," she said.

"Lax, please, I will eat, but don't ask me to go anywhere. I am sorry I won't let you win on this."

"Akka, please, not for you but for me. I need to buy clothes for my birthday plus for the New Year party." Lax said and left quickly, not wanting to hear a no.

After an hour Laxmi came to her room again and saw she was sleeping. She hated to do this, but she had to take her out.

"Akka! Don't do this, please. Okay, don't take a shower; just come with me. Nobody would know since you always look so fresh." She begged.

"Lax, please, I am sorry."

"Fine, okay, anyway, why would you listen to me? Who am I? It's okay; I give up." Lax said, and Arannya turned to the other side.

"Just wanted to remind you that when you came back from home and didn't get me anything, you promised to owe me one. Today I want you to do that. If you choose not to, I will know my place and won't ever ask you for anything." Lax played her last emotional card, and it worked.

Arannya asked her to pick clothes for her and got ready. They went to the same mall where she went for a movie with Ray. She couldn't tell Laxmi that she was feeling suffocated. Laxmi took her to different shops and bought clothes for herself. She insisted Arannya try something, but she refused. After her shopping, Arannya asked if they could leave, but Lax was acting weird and was reluctant to leave. She said she's hungry, and they went to the food court. Lax knew Arannya was hating this, but she was doing this for her.

They struggled to find a place at the food court. Arannya was irritated, but her goody two-shoes self didn't allow her to snap at Lax. Arannya, still unable to find a place, was standing and waiting for Lax to place the order and come back. After struggling for 15 minutes, Lax came to her and said it's too crowded, and she'll have coffee instead. The cafe was on the ground floor, and while coming down on escalators, Arannya saw Ray with *her*.

Ray, along with his wife, was checking something in the canopy store placed in the middle of the mall. Arannya asked Lax to go ahead in the coffee shop, and she'll join her later. She meticulously lurked around them; Ray did not notice her. She noticed his wife; she was a beautiful-looking woman with long, brown, curly hair, milky skin, and golden-brown eyes. They complimented each other splendidly.

Arannya was behind them, dying every second watching them together. This is his life; she wanted to make her heart feel the pain in an attempt to let go of her feelings towards him. And then Ray saw her. He was composed and did not panic; Arannya could have confronted him there and ruined it for him. But being a trouble to him was still the last thing on her mind.

Albeit their heart shattered, the symphony of their pain was such that this moment was no less than the sad song of their life.

And then Ray realised why exactly he orchestrated this juncture and played his move. Maintaining steady eye contact with Arannya, he held his wife's hand, pulled her closer, and whispered something in her ear. She giggled and knocked him from her elbow. And then they hugged. Ray, still maintaining eye contact with Arannya as if he wanted to show how happy he was, succeeded in ripping her heart apart. He strangled her from afar, but she could feel the choke physically. She clenched her top's collar and ran away from there. Lax, who was noticing everything, looked at Ray in ambivalence and went after her.

"Akka, Akka, wait!" Lax ran behind her.

"Laxmi, I want to meet Gautam right now," she said adamantly.

"Sure, Akka, let me get the car."

Gautam, who was busy shooting, got a call from Lax, and she told him Arannya wanted to meet him. He said he'll come to their place right after his shoot, but Arannya said she can't wait. They reached the studio; he was giving his shot. After the director's cut, he came rushing towards them and asked what's the matter. Arannya asked if he could come aside, as she needed to speak to him. He agreed and took her to a vanity van.

"What's the matter, Aaru?" Gautam made her sit and asked.

She showed him her left hand in which she wore his ring and said, "Let's get married!"

Gautam was so overjoyed that he ran out of words and hugged her.

"But…" she said and paused,

"But what?" he retracted.

"I have one request," she said. "We have to get married within a month,"

"That's the cherry on top, darling!" Gautam said and hugged her again.

She accepted her defeat and gave up on her feelings towards Ray.

This news spread across Arannya's office like a wildfire; people started to come and congratulate her. Some of them were starstruck when they heard she was going to marry an actor. Ray prayed for this to happen. He knew Arannya would never give up on him, and only something drastic could make her do that. She was an impulsive decision maker, and Ray banked on that.

New Year was approaching, and so was her wedding. Since Gautam and Arannyas' home towns were two worlds apart, they decided to get married in the city where they were working. Their parents agreed to it, while Arannya's parents wanted to make it a cosmic event; Arannya wanted to keep it a personal affair and invite only the close family members. Lax and her friends helped in securing a villa that was generally used for shoots. Gautam was excited and took an active part in the arrangements; Arannya, however, was just counting the number of days left until Ray's last working day. Her motive behind getting married within a month was to show Ray she's moved on too.

Ray, who behaved unbothered and ignored Arannya, started to steal a few glances at her. He knew these were the last few days when they still were under the same roof.

Lax was trying to keep herself from telling Arannya about the conversation she had with Ray on the call the other day.

One of the days, around lunchtime, Dinesh came to Sujith and gave him an invitation card.

"What? Are you getting married again?" Sujith mocked.

"I am not that lucky. It's my elder brother's second marriage. Do come along with your Narayan sir. Ummm, by the way, I invited him *with his family*." Dinesh winked. He was pointing at Ray's wife. Sujith turned around and saw Ray; the card was kept beside him.

"How can a human stoop so low! Bloody leech!" Sujith cussed Dinesh as he left, ridiculing.

Arannya connected the dots that maybe since Dinesh's brother was getting married, Ray's wife came back to him! How can she be so selfish?! She thought about Ray and what he must be going through, but she never let him know that she knows about his wife; this will break her man's pride, and she never wanted that to happen.

Ray picked up the card and left from there. The reason for his wife's return was busted. He wanted to go and throw the card in her face. Ray was already coping with her infidelity, but he realised he does not deserve this humiliation he faces in the office because of her. He drove rashly that evening and reached home. As soon as she opened the door, he threw the card on her face.

"Is this why you came back to me?" He screamed.

"All these years I kept up with your cheating and thought one day you would realise and come clean, and that day when you did, I thought maybe, finally, my life would be normal and I wouldn't suffocate anymore! But no! You came back to me because he left you!" His rage escalated. "Why? Why did you do this to me? Why!? And when I finally mended my heart and started to live on my own, you came and snatched that peace too away from me." He fell on the floor and cried. His wife was speechless; she had already lost her defence; in fact, she was already his criminal, living under his courtesy and forbearance.

"I am sorry, Ray." She apologised. But Ray had had enough, and he just wanted to break free from this muck.

"Enough! Enough of your sorries. I want a divorce!" He shouted.

"What?! No." His wife's voice was shaking. "No, no, Ray, you can't do this!" She pleaded,

"Of course I can; I can't be with you and your deceit. You are free to do whatever you want, but I can't deal with you anymore! I am done." He was determined.

"Ha ha ha ha ha, he he he he, huh, ha ha ha, divorce!" She started to laugh hysterically. Her behaviour left Ray horrified.

"You think you can leave me easily?" Her tone changed dramatically. "Sure, go ahead. But remember, if you leave me, I will never let Krishaan see you ever again!" She threatened. Ray was taken aback. It was at this moment that he knew he was doomed. Not only will she take his son away from him, but she will ruin his and his family's life; she belonged to a powerful family ultimately. Her family has helped Ray's family financially when they faced losses in their business. If it's for her, she can go to any extent. Looking at his vulnerable state, she chuckled and said, "Let's keep things going as is. You'll come to terms with it, won't you, honey?" She sat next to him, held his hand, and rested her head on his shoulder. Ray closed his eyes and wept silently. He has been mentally and emotionally abused by his wife earlier, but this time she was vehemently unapologetic about it. Which meant she feared nothing; she'd not even bother to pretend to be a good wife, and he was a puppet to her desires. This was his life.

Over a month was left for him to move to the states, and Arannya's wedding was planned a week before that. Arannya thought of speaking to him, but remembering the time she saw him in the mall with his wife and that look in his eyes shook her up.

It was the festive season, and everyone was in a merry mood. The new year was commencing, and like every year, the company's annual party was planned a day before Christmas. Everyone was invited with their partners. The invitation card, along with a sweet box, was distributed to all. Neither Ray nor Arannya was interested in going. But Ray's wife found the box along with the invite card in it and said, "This is exciting! We are going!" she exclaimed.

"Yes, you can go if you wish to, but don't expect me to come," he said.

"But why? Wouldn't it be amazing to meet your colleagues and know your secrets?" she said sarcastically and winked. "Or are you afraid I might just find something?" she asked.

"Don't compare me to yourself!" He snapped back at her and went to the washroom to freshen up. He knew her well and wanted to avoid any mano-a-mano between her and Arannya. He came out and went to the kitchen. "Haven't you cooked anything?" he asked. "Don't worry; the food is on the way," she replied. It's been weeks since he has eaten outside food. He got irritated and started to prepare dinner. "What are you doing?" she asked. "What does it look like?" he scorned. She ignored it and continued watching TV. "Prepare extra for me too," she ordered. "And yes, I want to go to that party, and then the next day we will visit Krishu." She said in a condescending manner. Ray was dying inside; he wanted to kill himself, but taking such a step at this point in time would do no good to anyone. Arannya has already endured the loss of her lover; he did not want to completely destroy her mental well-being. All he wished for was for her to get married and live a life she deserved. Because in this lifetime the only thing he could bring to the table for her was destruction.

Arannya, who had made up her mind not to attend the party, had a change of heart after knowing Ray would be there. She got to know this from the RSVP list. And this time she wanted to give him a taste of his own medicine.

December is a month of reminiscing about the entire year. It brings with it lots of pain and grief about what one has lost, what one couldn't achieve, the broken hopes, and despair. Lies and deceit. With its deadly freezing temperature, it makes people miss the ones they love who are away from each other and makes those who are near come even closer. It's like the ending sequence of any random Indian film, where all the characters in the plot gather together for a happy ending, and if the ending is not a happy one, then it's really not the end.

Apart from lingering grief, December also marks the foundation of new aspirations and hopes for the upcoming year. For Arannya, it was filled with sorrow but also a lot of will to take the leap of faith into the unknown.

It was the 24th of December, and the company has announced a half day for everyone to go home early and get ready for the party. Arannya has taken a long leave from then until February. Ray's LWD was on 20th January, four days before her wedding, and he was flying abroad in the first week of February. So officially it was Arannya's and Ray's last day together in the office.

The previous night, Ray and Sujith had drinks together. Ray wasn't feeling like going to his place, and he insisted Sujith accompany him. Sujith obliged. Both of them went to a local bar and ordered a bottle of Old Monk. Sujith knew something was wrong with him and waited for him to speak. Ray kept quiet till the last peg was made from the bottle.

"I love her, Sujith." Ray confessed.

"I know, sir," Sujith replied casually.

"Hey! We're out of the office; drop the titles." Ray commanded.

"Sorry, Bhai." Sujith smiled.

"By the way, how do you know whom I am talking about?"

"Isn't it obvious, Bhai? It's Arannya."

"How! How could it be so obvious?"

"Have you ever seen yourself while you were around her or talking to her? Everything changes in you; you have a constant smile on your otherwise grim face. Also, since she started to be a part of our group, you've screwed us considerably less at work." Sujith said and bit his tongue.

"Watch it now!"

"Uhh, sorry,"

"Just kidding." Ray laughed it off.

"But it's true, you know I have never experienced this feeling of being in love before Arannya came into my life. She has given me the taste of pure love, the elixir of the soul, which otherwise I would have been deprived of all my life." Ray stated.

"I second that," agreed Sujith.

They spoke about themselves until another bottle was poured half. Sujith also knew he had very few days left with Ray; he wanted to apologise for telling Arannya about Ray's miserable married life.

"Bhai, I wanted to seek your apology for something I am guilty of." Sujith said.

"What is it?" Ray asked as he rotated his glass while deep in Arannya's thoughts.

"That day when you left the office after the spat with Dinesh over the potluck thing, she was worried and was calling you but couldn't reach you. So..." Sujith said and paused.

"So?" Ray asked.

"So I told her about you, like the whole thing. and she started to cry; I was amused. Why is this girl crying? As if she has been through all the humiliation along with you. In case you were wondering how she knows about you."

"She knows?" Ray was surprised.

"She knows." Sujith affirmed.

"Wait, you mean hasn't she never confronted you?" Even Sujith was surprised.

"Never." Ray became pensive.

Ray was hurt, mostly guilty; he blamed himself for giving her such a hard time, while even after knowing everything, she said nothing to him, just to keep his pride high in her eyes. How could she be a decade younger than him and still be so sensible? Age really is just a number. He felt like calling her and apologising for behaving like a jerk. But it was too late in the night, and he dropped the idea.

The next day, Arannya was teary-eyed since morning; she cried her heart out before coming to the office. Ray's situation was no different. They knew this was it; it was the last day for them to be around each other. While driving to the office, both of them crossed 'Ferrum Mount' and got reminded of the beautiful times they had spent there. Ray saw Arannya's car and parked his car next to hers. He glided his fingers on the dust of her car's glass. He wanted to see her; the fact that she knew everything about him and chose not to confront him moved him. So he straight away went to her floor instead. She wasn't there. "Where's Arannya?" he asked Vrushabh. "I don't know; she came a while ago, kept her bag, and went somewhere," he answered. Disheartened, he went back to his floor. What he was thinking he couldn't understand, but today he wanted to see her, talk to her, apologise to her.

"Good morning, Ray!" Pulkit from his team greeted him. "Morning!" he replied.

"By the way, Miss. Arannya came looking for you." Pulkit informed.

"Really?" Ray was instantly adrenalised. "What did she say? Never mind," he said, and left from there in search of her. He went to the coffee bay, rec area, and even back to her floor but couldn't find her. He was striding like someone high on substance. "Cafeteria!" he exclaimed and pressed the elevator button ferociously. When it took long, he resorted to climbing the stairs. He was panting, but the eagerness to know why she came looking after him infused a teenage vigour in him. "Huh huh huh," he was gasping. As he reached the cafeteria, he saw her; she was waiting near the lift.

"Arannyaaaaaa," he literally shouted her name.

She looked at him; "At last," she mouthed; she was glued to the ground. In that moment of emotional catharsis, she just wanted to run towards him and dig in his arms. But the ogling eyes around provided enough resistance.

"Hi!" He greeted her as he walked up to her.

"Hey!" she responded.

"You came looking for me?" he asked.

"Yes," she replied.

"Yeah, tell me?" He was excited.

"Nothing, just wanted to give you this. You are the first person I am inviting to my wedding. 24th January, do come." She said and handed him a pocket-size wedding card. AG were the initials printed on a small plastic tag in the shape of wings and glued on the top of the card.

"That's all?" he asked.

"Yeah!" she said and left. She wanted to go back and hug him; she knew that had hurt him. But at least for once she has to be headstrong and overpower her heart's emotion. And today she did it. A current of strong, sad emotion ran through Ray. He was left stunned.

She went back to her floor, and Vrushabh told her he came looking after her twice. She asked when. Samar from the next row answered as soon as he came to the office and then again after 5 minutes. He wanted to see me?! And I totally screwed it. What do I do now? Should I go back to him? She had these thoughts. She became anxious. Should I go and talk to him now? She thought. But then her phone got a notification: Team Dailies in 15 minutes. She took her laptop and headed towards the conference room. She was getting nervous; she wanted the meeting to finish quickly so that she could run to him. But the meeting took three hours to conclude. As soon as the meeting got over, she rushed to his floor; everyone was packing their stuff and were about to leave. She went to his place, but he wasn't there.

"Did he leave?" she asked Pulkit.

"Yes, a while ago,"

"Shit!" She exclaimed and ran to the parking lot.

"What's with these guys today?" Pulkit wondered.

"Arannya," somebody called her; it was Sujith. She did not stop; he ran behind her. By the time she reached the parking lot, she saw his car had just made the exit. She was sweating and panting.

"What happened, Aaru? You alright?" Sujith asked.

"Yeah, no, actually. Ray wanted to talk to me, but…" She said and stopped.

"But?" he asked.

"Nothing, let's leave. I will get my bag," she said.

It was a very important night for Arannya and Ray, as they won't be seeing each other after tonight. Arannya wanted to look her best since she might bump into his wife at the party; she did not want to look any lesser than her. Gautam was excited to accompany Arannya as her partner. As this would be their first public appearance together, he wanted to look his best too. Ray's wife booked the salon in the morning and got her diamond necklace from the locker. Ray felt like a jilted lover, dejected by Arannya. He had no will to show up, but his wife had the final word. She has already picked clothes for him to twin.

Arannya and Ray were hurt, sad, and pensive. Will he speak to her again after her cold behaviour? Both of them had the same question.

Arannya called Gautam, "Hey! What time will you be free?" she asked

"By 8:30, Master, but I will try to be there before that," he replied.

"Okay, let me know," she said and hung up.

She went to the mall and bought a red, backless, cowl-neck silk gown and went to the hair and makeup studio to get ready. At 6, after an hour, she dialled Gautam again. He did not answer. *'Ting,'* she got a message from him.

"Master, I'll be a bit late. Please go ahead, and I will join you shortly. Send me the live location too." Gautam requested.

Arannya wasn't bothered; all she could think was to show her best self to Ray. She carried her bags and managed to walk fast in the brand new stilettos. As she was walking towards her car, Gautam came and grabbed her from behind. She was startled!

"Drop-dead gorgeous!" He whispered in her ear.

"When do you come?" She was surprised.

"I was here the whole time," his smile reached his ears. He came only a while ago after she shared her location.

"You give your bags to me and keep your car here. I will get my car." He said and went to get his car.

"But one thing is missing," he said as she sat in the car.

"what?" she asked.

"Your neck looks empty; I wish I could tie a *mangalsutra* right away!" He winked. "Never mind; till then you'll have to make do with this." He said and reached his hands in the back seat to take a bag.

"Close your eyes and turn around," he requested.

He placed an emerald necklace over her neck.

"You may open your eyes," he whispered in her ear.

"This is so beautiful! Thank you, Gautam." She thanked him.

"But it comes with a cost." He said, Arannya was puzzled. He held her hand and asked, "May I?" She nodded, and he planted a kiss.

And suddenly she was taken back to the time with Ray in the car when they were going for the trip. He did not even ask and just kissed her, which in turn melted her like wax.

Whereas Gautam, like a true gentleman, asked for her permission, leaving her feeling awkward. She was comfortable with Ray, who was somebody else's man, and felt uneasy when her own fiancé did it.

"What happened?" he noticed as she zoned out.

"Nothing, we're getting late; let's go."

"Your wish is my command!" he said and blew a chef's kiss.

They reached the venue about an hour late. The party started, and people were already high on the cocktails. Gautam gave keys to the valet, and they went inside.

"This way, sir," the hotel staff guided them. "Hi, Arannya!" Sharanya came and greeted her. She was rather interested in Gautam. "Hi Gautam! Such a huge fan of your show." She had a little fan moment there. Those who knew Arannya all gathered around to have a selfie with

Gautam. She went to greet her manager. And her eyes were scanning the entire ballroom. It was a beautiful golden-themed ballroom, with carefully placed handpicked artefacts and a huge red carpet hugging the floor. A mini pond with various colours of fish cohabiting made Arannya wonder, Are fish the most beautiful creatures, or birds? But the centre of attraction was the humongous golden crystal chandelier, which gave it the feel of a royal palace. Gautam, given his nature, became comfortable quickly and was exchanging words with the director. Where was he? She couldn't find him. Even Sujith was nowhere to be found. She dialled Sujith. "Where on earth are you?" she asked. "In the bar lounge, give me 5," he said and hung up before she could ask her next question. She requested the waiter to get her champagne and went to meet and greet her team. Sujith came after a couple of minutes. "Hey! Gorgeous!" He said and hugged her. "You've made up your mind to kill Ray today, I see!" He was clearly drunk. "Shhh," she shushed him. Gautam came, and she introduced them to each other.

"So sad to hear about your loss," Sujith said to Gautam.

"Sorry?" Gautam was perplexed.

"You must have lost your mind to marry her," Sujith said, and they burst out laughing.

"Arannya was right about you! It's so nice to meet you, brother." Gautam shook his hand and side-hugged him.

"Likewise!" Sujith replied. Arannya felt like punching Sujith. She pulled Sujith aside and asked, "When they are serving drinks here, why the hell do you go to the bar, idiot?" She said, gnashing her teeth and maintaining a robotic smile.

"Two reasons: one, my big brother Ray is leaving the company, so I'm sad, and two…" He stopped in between and looked straight into Arannya's eyes. Arannya got shivers down her spine. What if he says something stupid?

"And two?" asked Gautam.

"And two… who the hell gets high on free whisky! Hahaha." "Phew," Arannya sighed as she escaped by the skin of her teeth.

"There he is! Long live Narayan Bhaiya!" Sujith exclaimed as he saw Ray enter the room.

"Who is Narayan?" Gautam asked.

"Ray." She said in a voice audible only to her ears as her jaw dropped seeing Ray in all black. The director, who was fascinated by Gautam, called him, and he left from there. Arannya was so awestruck that she completely turned deaf when Gautam said he'll be back in a moment. This was her moment; the love of her life was in front of her! Looking like an absolute piece of her favourite dessert. And the tuxedo made him look irresistible to her. The duet of soft music on the centralised speakers and heavy beats of the DJ created a whole new symphony. And when he saw her looking at him, it was as if the world around them went blurry. The spotlight was on them, the music in their ears faded away, and faces around them melted away. They walked towards each other, looked into each other's eyes, and let them do the talking. When their emotions were conveyed telepathically, a drop of tear fell from Arannya's eye, and before it could fall on the ground, Ray caught it on his lips, and they kissed. As if they were only two under the huge chandelier, as if nobody noticed them, and even if they did, they did not give two cents about it and just kissed.

"Arannya... Arannya," she could hear someone calling her name in a faint voice. Someone shook her. It was Samar. "Huh," she was flustered. It was a dream, she saw with her open eyes. "What?" she asked him, but her eyes were glued to Ray and his dimples. Few people from his team were gathered around him. And when they cleared off, she understood the reason. They were there to meet Mrs. Narayan. Arannya saw *her*. She was wearing a black saree, perfect figure, perfect height. Golden hair complimenting her brown eyes and milky skin. She was looking no less than a deadly attractive dark feminine damsel. Till now Ray did not see Arannya.

"Ray bhai, have you seen her yet? She is looking killer; even my intentions are shaking!" A drunk Sujith told Ray. Ray smiled in response. As his wife was around.

"Who?" His wife asked Sujith.

"Someone he has a crush on." Ray interrupted.

"Let's go meet the director," Ray said to Sujith.

"I am not going to stick with you. You wanted to come to the party; here we are. Now spare me." He said in her ears. And she flaunted a smile as if he was telling her something funny.

"Oh! Look who's here! Hi, *Bhabiji,* Dinesh said as he walked towards them.

"I forgot you have a company here! Your brother-in-law." Ray taunted and left with Sujith.

"Okay, you drunken fool! Now tell me where she is." Ray asked.

"There she is!" Sujith pointed to her back, facing Ray. Ray noticed her bare back, all covered with body glitter, which still failed to compete with the mole on the lower right of her back. The golden chain straps have left their mark on the previous position from where they were moved. This must be hurting her, he thought. She has forgotten to remove the price tag completely from her brand-new pointed stilettos. Will she be able to carry them properly? Why does she have to wear heels and hurt her poor ankles?

"Here, brother, have this whisky. I have tipped the waiter heavily to pour single malt for us." Sujith said, and they cheered. Ray took the bottoms up. Then she turned around. And left Ray mesmerised. Her curled hair made her look entirely different but only enhanced her beauty. She wore a rose gold watch on her right hand this time. Usually she wears it on her left, he noticed. The cowl neck amplified her otherwise hidden beautiful collarbones.

And the emerald necklace did all the justice to compliment her attire. There she was, the love of his life.

When finally their eyes met, they spoke all the unsaid feelings. They craved to hold each other. They both got high just by looking at each other. Both of them were experiencing wild emotions running through their bodies. They wanted to be in each other's embrace, but alas, the reality. Alas, the compulsion. Alas, their love.

Sharannya, who was swayed by Ray too, took to the stage. Jealous of the way Ray and Arannya drool over each other, she decided to steal some attention from Arannya.

"Guys! Today let me spill out a secret!" Everyone turned towards her. "What is she up to?!" Samar exclaimed.

"We have a very talented writer amongst us. Can anyone guess?" she asked the audience. Few names came up along with Ray's.

"Yes, it's none other than Ray! I got this honour to accompany him on a trip and listen to some great lines he has written. Still stuck in my mind." She said, and everyone started to hoot; her affection towards Ray has always been an open book.

"When I catch you looking at me,

I wonder how it could be?

Time stops, and so do we.

and the realm is only me and thee."

Sharannya recited a couplet written by Ray.

"To Ray, everyone!" she said and gestured to everyone to clap. "And along with this I have a request to Ray to please come on stage and share a few of your lines with us. And we HR don't take no for an answer from people on notice period." She said, and everyone laughed.

"HRs should also be stand-up comedians now!" Samar came and said to Arannya.

"Well, isn't she great?" she asked.

"Oh, she's a natural." Samar said while everyone clapped as Ray walked on stage.

"Thank you, Sharannya. I really appreciate that you remember what I wrote." He said.

"Okay, so I don't want to bore you guys and be done with it quickly. This is something I have written lately, and any similarity to any person is purely intentional." He said and saw his wife, who was sitting and sipping her wine. Everyone cheered him up.

"I don't know what you are to me.

a lost lover of the past,

or some karmic melancholy!

It hurts to think, what if we were never meant to be?

I guess we are star-crossed lovers.

Let's end this agony!"

Everyone in the room became silent. His wife knew he pointed to a separation.

He continued.

"Let's end this agony;

for we know we don't belong in this world.

Let's break free from the decorum.

And be on the run.

For you and I know better,

that our hearts dwell inside one another!"

He finished his lines. Looked at Arannya, let the single malt act upon him, and confessed,

"I love you."

People were busy clapping and appreciating; his wife was on top of the world. But Arannya knew he wrote it for her. This was the first time he said those three magical words to her in front of so many people disguised under his wife's presence.

He came down and walked towards Arannya and Gautam.

"Congratulations, Gautam! You are a lucky man." He congratulated him.

"And so are you." Gautam said and tilted his head towards Ray's wife.

Ray badged a miserable smile. His wife joined in.

"Hi Gautam! It's surprising to me that you guys know each other. Ray never mentioned it?"

"Actually, we know each other through my wife. Oh, fiancé, I mean." Gautam said as he held Arannya by her shoulders and narrowed his eyes while looking at Ray's changing expressions.

"Interesting! Tell me more," his wife asked. Ray and Arannya thought Gautam might tell his wife that she was at his place once, but Gautam dropped the subject saying, "Long story some other time. And I hope you got our wedding invite; do come!"

"Baby, do you need anything? I am going to get myself a drink." Gautam asked Arannya.

"Yeah, sure," she said, and they walked off.

Ray saw he was holding Arannya from her waist, and a sense of jealousy ran through him. He was already furious to hear him call her his wife; seeing this made him fume with anger and envy.

After a while somebody announced a paper dance competition. The couples were requested to actively participate. Ray told the team he got a sprain in his leg and opted out.

Gautam and Arannya, along with ten other couples, participated in the game. The host asked the controller to start the music. Arannya was shying away from holding Gautam in front of Ray; she knew this would hurt him. But she wanted to show him that this will be her life now. And he has to accept this harsh truth like she had.

In the first fold, Gautam held her hands, and they started to tap their feet in the rhythm of the beats. In the second fold they came a little closer, but their bodies were not touching yet. She kept her hands on his shoulders, and he was snapping his fingers from both his hands. In this round three couples were eliminated from the competition. In the third round, as the fold became smaller, they had to hug each other to survive the round. Gautam held Arannya closer; Ray saw that Gautam slid his hands inside her dress, which were touching her stomach.

More than being angry, Ray was sad, hurt, and in pain to see the love of his life looking so beautiful dancing in another man's arms. The music began, and they started to move carefully. The remaining couple in this round seemed to be great at their game. It was more than two minutes, and they were all playing well. The host asked to play a sensual song, and the lights were dimmed. Ray was choked with emotions while looking at Arannya. Why has life been so unfair towards them? He was trying hard to hide his tears. And when he saw Gautam planting a kiss on her cheeks, he lost it. He kept his glass on the table and strode towards them. Took Arannya's left hand, slid his right hand from her wrist, and intertwined the fingers. Made eye contact with her, and she knew she had to go with him.

He was leading the way out, and she was following him. No questions asked. Breaking all the relations, walking with the love of her life.

They waged a lifelong war with this move, but is there a great love without waging one?

Gautam took Arannya's phone and bag and left the party. Ray's wife faced the humiliation of all the eyes watching her, few pitifully and more ridiculing.

This was an astounded display of their love saga, which they kept under wraps for so long. But nature has its way to show up when it's due. And the 'truth' is that element that cannot be kept suppressed for long. They were soulmates, past-life lovers, twin flames, or two bodies, one soul—who knows? But their souls were home to each other.

Coming out of the ballroom, Ray took her to the reception.

"Hi! We haven't made any reservations and are too tired; can you please arrange a room for us?" he asked.

Arannya was unable to fathom what just happened.

"Sorry, sir, but all our rooms are booked at the moment. Only the President suite is available," replied the receptionist.

"Okay, here's my card. Can I get the key, please?" He said. She swiped the card for an amount of half a lakh and gave him the keycard.

They went inside the elevator; she held his hand; it was hot, and hers was ice cold. They reached their floor.

He unlocked the door, still holding her hand from another hand, and walked inside the room. As the door got locked, he held her face with both his hands, looked in her eyes until he saw his own reflection, and kissed her forehead. He then kneeled on the floor and cried like a baby. She was standing there, speechless. He held her feet, bent his head, and cried. Cried because he knew he loved her, cried because he knew she loved him, cried because they cannot be together. His tears touched her feet. She also kneeled. Held his face in her hand and saw him with broken tears flooding out of his eyes. This shattered her heart into a million pieces. Her throat was choked up. She wasn't able to say a word seeing him so fragile and broken like this. Tears started to roll from her eyes, but she lost her tongue. Ray kept crying endlessly as if all the water in his body was pouring out in his tears.

He took her hands and saw her palms as if he was searching for some specific lines there that indicated their love, kissed them, rested his head in them, and sobbed perpetually. She caressed his hair and kissed his hair and gestured not to cry, but all he did was cry, cry, and cry. Arannya realised how much he loved her. She was happy to know this and cried in both grief and joy. But she did not know there's more to it; Ray has decided to take his life as soon as she is married. And this was his final goodbye to her.

They hugged and cried, holding each other in different ways as if they were finding a position to get locked forever in each other's embrace.

They didn't say a word. But their souls were connected in such a manner that they were not prisoners of words to communicate. The air around them, the eye glances, the loud and silent tears, the soft and hard grip of the hands, and the warm and tight hugs were enough to penetrate through their hearts and convey what they felt for each other.

It was 4 am in the morning. They were still on the room's floor hugging each other and hadn't moved an inch. As if they didn't want to spend even a second apart from whatever time was left with them. The beautiful suite witnessed two lovers for the first time. They did not care to look around the ravishing work of art that the room was, but each other. "That's true love," said the bed to its other inanimate roommates as it sobbed.

They checked out around 5 am. Arannya noticed her phone and bag were left at the party. Ray turned his phone on and saw trails of missed calls, messages, and voice notes from his wife, Gautam, Sujith, and a few of his colleagues.

His phone buzzed again. It was his wife. He rejected the call.

Neither she nor he cared about what was going to happen when they walked out last night.

Ray checked Gautam's message; it read, "Keep her safe. I trust you, Man!"

This was that breather for him that he wasn't expecting. Ray saw Gautam in a different light; he was relieved to know Gautam is such a gem of a person.

He came to drop her off at her place. She was ready to let go of Gautam and apologise to him for putting him down.

She rang the doorbell, and Gautam rushed and opened the door for her. He saw Ray and then saw Arannya.

"Gautam, I am so sorry..." she apologised.

"Thank God you are a safe baby. I was so worried!" Gautam said and hugged her.

"Thank you, Ray! For always keeping her safe." He thanked him.

Ray and Arannya were puzzled by his behaviour; in any world, this isn't normal. But Ray sighed in relief knowing Gautam is the person who will look after her.

"Gautam, I want to tell you something." Arannya said.

"Can this wait?" he asked. "No," she said and took him to the balcony.

"Gautam, I don't understand how you could be so cool about everything. After what happened last night, I thought you'd call our wedding off. I know I should be the one answerable, but this thing is troubling me to an extent that my heart is drowning in guilt," she said and continued. "I had told you the other day that I wouldn't be able to reciprocate love, and hence I want to marry someone who doesn't want it either. But I hid one thing from you, and I feel this is necessary for you to know because I don't want to ruin your life. I love Ray," she confessed.

"I know," he said.

"What? Since when?" She was taken aback.

"Maybe from the very beginning," he said and continued, "You remember the first time I stayed over and everyone was over drunk. That day when you took Lax to her room, I followed you thinking you might need some help and heard her saying, *"It doesn't matter if he's married; if it makes you happy, I am with you."* Then after a few months, when Ray took you to his place when you had a vertigo, it took me seconds to realise Ray is that person. And when Ray insisted I come to his place, I could feel it in my heart that he's a genuine man. So even after knowing you loved him, it never bothered me; in fact, I was pitiful towards you, Aaru, and knew you would need me. Even if you don't, I would be by your side. No matter what." He said.

Arannya was in complete disbelief; there was a time in her life when she craved love. And now here she is with these two men who love her better than she imagined.

"I still just have one question for you: Will you let me love you?" He asked. She was guilty as she wasn't used to being on the favourable side of her fate. She turned around and saw Ray. He was talking to Lax. "Do you need his permission?" he asked. "No," she said. "So it's a yes then?" he asked. She nodded. "Come on now, give me a hug." He pulled her in and hugged her.

They came inside the room; Ray was sitting with his head resting on his folded hands. "Your prayers are answered, lucky man!" Gautam said, and Ray saw Arannya with teary eyes.

"I'll take my leave now," said Ray. He got up, and Gautam asked if he could ride him home. "No, you guys need rest. I know sorry wouldn't make up for the trouble I caused, but please forgive me." Ray sought his apologies.

Gautam hugged him and whispered in his ear, "I am going to make sure that this is the last time you are seeing her." He squeezed him.

Ray wasn't surprised, as this is how any sane person would behave if they happened to meet their fiancée's lover. Ray saw her one last time before he left. He could feel it in his heart that this is the last time he is seeing her. Probably the last time talking to her too.

Gautam's behaviour was godly. He did not create a ruckus; instead, he dealt with the situation, keeping the dignity of his women intact. Arannya, still in disbelief, was trying to make sense out of it. Gautam genuinely loved her so much that he kept his ego aside and let this slide. But there was one thing he had kept hidden from the world till now, about his sexuality. And Arannya's situation was exactly what he wanted it to be.

No other girl would ever understand his situation, but Arannya would, as he has now done her a favour.

Gautam was asexual.

The next day, Arannya's parents arrived at her place. And Gautam's amicable nature made them extremely happy. "Good mor-noon." It was half past 12; Gautam greeted Arannya and asked if she needed rest; they could postpone it for the next day. She was already under a lot of guilt and did not want to take undue advantage of Gautam's care towards her.

"Our wedding is only weeks away; each day matters." Arannya said.

"Plus, tomorrow never comes, and yesterday never happened," Gautam added and told her he will go to his place to get ready, pick up his parents, and come back to pick them up.

Arannya said she would get her car, but Gautam asked her not to drive. He had a seven-seater SUV. Their parents were meeting each other for the first time but instantly became like a family. Gautam's father was sitting at the front when they arrived. His father insisted Arannya's father sit in the front, and he can manage in the back seat. Arannya's father declined politely and said he and her mom will sit comfortably at the back, and Arannya and her mother-in-law can sit in the middle. Seeing this, Gautam's mom said, We two old ladies would sit in the middle; you two oldies go at the back and let the bride and groom take the front seat. Everyone agreed with the arrangement, and Gautam drove off.

They first went to buy the jewellery and then their wedding dresses. Gautam knew Arannya was trying her best to gel in, but her eyes failed to hide her hurt. They went to the studio and tried different clothes. Arannya was okay with everything, and Gautam was genuinely showing interest. There came a moment when she tried an ivory and golden colour lehenga; this was Ray's favourite colour since he loved white and its shades. She looked at herself in the mirror. The intricate golden and red zardozi work was perfectly handcrafted. When the salesperson draped the dupatta over her shoulder, she was awestruck by how beautiful it was looking on her, as if it was bespoke for her. She daydreamed about wearing that and walking towards Ray someday. Gautam came and nudged her from his shoulder and asked, 'What?' nonverbally by raising both his eyebrows and tossing his head up. "Nothing," she shook her head in response.

"Mom, Dad, we can finalise these." Gautam said.

The next few days were spent shopping. Gautam's parents asked for an engagement. But Arannya was of the opinion of getting married straight away. This would save her from the guilt at least for one time. Gautam made his parents understand that their wedding was only a few weeks away and engagement wouldn't make sense. His parents got upset and asked if he was under any kind of pressure, as they could now sense Arannya's disinterest. He brushed off all the allegations.

But Gautam knew the reason for her incuriousness. He took her for a pre-marriage counselling session; which proved to be helpful.

Only a week was left for their wedding. All the arrangements were made. Thanks to their friends. Lax was so busy in all of these that she did not get a chance to be with Arannya and talk for a minute. Arannya's nearest family started to arrive one by one. In her family, only her maternal aunt had a daughter, and the rest had sons. Her daughter was a decade older than Arannya, and she flew to India especially for her wedding from Salzburg, though she was apologetic that her husband and son couldn't make it. Everyone was busy with the preparations, but she was sceptical of Arannya's on-and-off behavior. At times she was excited about normal things and at times passed a very plain reaction to significant things. Since she was alone, she came and stayed with Arannya, and all the other guests were arranged to stay in the hotel.

"Aaru, you are sure about this, right?" Her sister asked.

"Yes, Didi, why did you ask so?"

"Nothing just like that. I'm happy for you, my little bird," she said.

Gautam called everyone and arranged for a cocktail party. He requested Arannya to wear the same dress she wore at the office party. Gautam invited all their friends and Sujith too. He wanted to officially propose to Arannya. Around 25 people were a part of that dinner. It was arranged in the same hotel their relatives were staying in.

They enjoyed various dishes of Italian, Lebanese, and Turkish cuisine. Men and a few women had no accountability on the number of Sauza gold shots they had. Gautam was four shots down, topped with a jager bomb. Arannya had a few shots along with her sister and Lax. Sujith came almost an hour late to the party.

"Welcome, Brooooo." Gautam went and hugged him. "We were all waiting for you." He said.

Sujith went to meet Arannya.

This was Arannya's chance to ask Ray's whereabouts. The moment Sujith was going to answer her, Gautam came and took her away. "Sorry, bro, I need to talk to my fiancée," and winked.

"Aarna, I want to talk to you. Can you come with me, please?"

He took her to one of the rooms where their relatives were checked in.

"What is it, Gautam?" she began to sweat.

What if he demands something out of her that she is not ready for? This thought was petrifying her.

"Is it necessary that we go inside the room? Can't we speak somewhere out? What if someone sees us? Mom and Dad are around too!" She was trying to convince him as their lift approached the 8th floor.

He did not say a word.

He unlocked the door and stood holding it for her to enter the room. The room's bed was filled with rose petals, but the wrinkles on the sheets witnessed that someone already made good use of it. He closed the door. She got scared and sat on the chair.

"Am I scaring you, baby?" he asked.

"No," she said and asked if she could drink some water. He opened the fridge, poured a glass for her, and sat on the bed. Few petals got stuck to his hands. "My cousins! I'll tell you," he said.

"Hmm," she faked a smile.

"Arannya,"

"Yes,"

"There's something that is eating me from inside as I have hidden it from you,"

"Just don't tell me that you killed someone; the rest is fine. Hahaha,"

"Aaru, this is serious."

"I am all ears, Gautam,"

"Arannya I promise to give you everything that you deserve and more. Whatever you wish for will be yours the next day. Except..." he stopped.

"Except?" she asked.

"Except for the fact that I can't consummate the marriage." He said it finally and closed his eyes. There were exactly 11 seconds of silence, and Arannya broke it by asking, "Are you into men?"

"What? No! I mean no offence to the ones who are, but how do I explain? I mean It's not that I can't copulate; it's like I don't feel like it."

Arannya took a few minutes to comprehend what she just heard and said, "Okay."

"Aaru, I am asexual!" Gautam emphasised the last word.

"Okay. That's alright," she said casually.

"Just okay? So you don't mind this?" He was curious.

"Why should I?" she asked and said, "Gautam, if you can accept me without love, why can't I accept you without sex? Wouldn't that be sheer hypocrisy from my end?" she asked.

"Aaru, this is not a joke." He was still in disbelief.

"I know," she said and lifted him from the bed for a friendly hug.

"I love you," he said.

"I know." She acknowledged.

"And I am sure one day I will win you over," he promised.

"I know that too," she said and retracted herself.

They went back to the party. Their parents and other elderly people left for their bed. Gautam lifted a wine glass, tapped the spoon to it, and made an announcement.

"Tonight is the best night of my life, as tonight I am officially putting a ring on my lady's finger."

He pulled out a magnanimous diamond ring and slipped it on her ring finger, along with the one she was already wearing, and planted a kiss on her forehead. Arannya's heart sank.

The next day, the Baratis were transported to the Villa. All the arrangements were made for the big day. It was the night of the Sangeet, followed by Mehandi and Haldi the next day before the wedding. Arannya, with a bruised and lost heart, was doing her best to not disappoint her family and Gautam at large, who had saved her from the misery of a pretentious life. Life wasn't that bad after all. She still gets to nurture her love for Ray in her heart, and seeing him happy after reconciling with his wife was enough for her to be at peace. But the most important moment was when he confessed his love towards her on the night of the annual party. She was content to know how much he loved her too. Doesn't that make her lucky? To know that someone you love loves you back tenfold more. Everyone was busy getting ready, and Arannya was made ready before everyone; she unconsciously kept checking her phone. She did not feel like talking to anyone; hence, she went out for a stroll. The resort was surrounded by hills on one side. It was getting chilly; the midday felt like late evening. Suddenly someone honked at her, and she turned around.

"Hey!" Sujith greeted and came out of the car.

She looked inside the car for Ray.

"There's no one inside!" Sujith said. She passed a miserable smile.

"By the way, before you officially become Mrs. From Miss. Can I take you for a coffee one last time?" He asked dramatically.

"What's with the theatrics?" She asked and sat in the car.

As cafes were not yet prominent in the tiny remote village, they went to a tea stall that was situated close to the cliff. They sat on the broken plastic chair, one with no hand and one with both hands tied by a copper wire, and a wooden stool kept in between.

"Such a beautiful view." Sujith said as he got two cups of tea. "Hmm," she responded.

They talked about random things related to wedding rituals, and Arannya could feel Sujith seemed a bit lost. "What's cooking in that brain of yours?" She asked. "Spit it out," she ordered.

"I am wondering why you haven't asked anything about Ray yet."

"What about him? He is happy in his life, and that's what I will always want. I hope he lives his best life wherever he plans to settle." She said and asked if he could get her another cup. Sujith called the child, probably the hawker's son, and asked him to get the tea for her.

"Arannya, I have a confession to make." Sujith said.

"Every time you say something in that tone, I know my life is doomed! Luckily we are at a perfect place; it will be a quick and easy death for me!" she said.

"Oh, shut up, Arannya!" he said angrily.

"Go on, tell me," she said calmly.

"Promise me you won't do anything stupid," he pleaded.

"There you go! Offers me poison and expects me to live! Of course I am not a teenager; now tell me." She said,

"The other day when I was drinking with Ray bhai, I didn't know you never confronted him about his marital situation, and I told him that you know everything," he said.

"What!" she was irked.

"It's not me; it's you who will die today! Why the fuck did you do that? When did you switch your role from Cupid to Anteros in my life?" She was angry.

"What are you saying? But I am sorry, Aaru. I never intended to, but I got lost in the conversation and told him."

"And what else do you tell him?"

"Let me get a cigarette first," he said and went to the stall.

"Get one for me too," she requested.

He got her one.

"Since when did you start to smoke?" he said and lit the cigarette for her.

"Since now." She took a drag and coughed.

"Anyway, I can't be bashing you like this, the Cupid of my life." She chuckled. "Everything is clear to me now; all I want is for him to be happy."

"He is not," Sujith said.

"What do you mean?" She looked straight into his eyes.

"Nothing, just forget it." He looked away.

"Swear on me, tell me." She kept his hand on her head.

"Don't make me do this, Aaru; he will kill me if he comes to know," he pleaded.

"I will kill you before that." She wasn't joking.

"He is being abused by his wife," he said.

"What do you mean?" asked Arannya, still trying to believe what he said.

Sujith told her how Ray is being abused by his wife, how she is torturing him. He told her Ray wanted a divorce, but she used their son as bait and told him she will never let him meet him and destroy his family.

He was a victim of domestic abuse, but unfortunately he wasn't entitled to justice in the eyes of our judiciary. Reason being, his gender.

She tortures him, asks him to have sex with her, and when he doesn't consent, she bites his private part and abuses him for being unable to do anything. He has been facing her mental abuse for a long time, but recently, after she learnt her lover was getting married again elsewhere, she has just lost it. And on the night of our party, when he left with you, she abused him physically too, accusing him of cheating. He kept apologising when she said she would destroy you using her father's political power. She has even run a background check on you and dug up some dirt against your parents' cases. He begged her not to do so and that he would do exactly as it pleases her.

She knew you were getting married and asked him to take her here. She wanted him to see how it feels when someone you love leaves you for another. He told her that Ray and his wife would be coming to her wedding.

"When Bhai told me all this, I felt like going and strangling that bitch myself. But Ray is powerless as his family and even his son's life are at stake." Sujith said.

"He loves you, Aaru," he concluded.

She was numb and shocked and angry and helpless. How she wished she could run to Ray and take him away with her to a safe place. How she wished that his wife should die in some accident and leave him be!

"You know what he said when I asked him not to attend your wedding just to satisfy that bitch's ego?"

"Let me live the experience of dying," Sujith told.

"You are his life, Arannya, and the only thing that will keep him happy is seeing you happy. Period."

This was the testament of their love, where both of them wanted just one thing: that the other should be happy, even if it wasn't with them.

It was the Haldi ceremony the next day. Being happy will make him happy, considering that Arannya held herself together and diverted her focus to the rituals. Maybe after his wife sees her getting married happily, she will cut some slack for Ray.

When Mehdi was being applied to her, her phone chimed with a message notification; Gautam was sitting alongside.

It was from Ray; Arannya sighed as she did not want to ruin Gautam's mood at the moment. But she got anxious to read his message. She wanted to be done with the mehendi and unlock her phone.

After a while, someone called Gautam, and he left from there. He was done with his mehendi, as men usually keep it simple. Arannya asked the henna artist to pick up the phone for her, and she unlocked it with her face. 'Hey

Buddy! open Inbox' She commanded the phone. 'Opening inbox,' the phone said. She tapped his message from her index finger and saw he had sent her his ticket's picture. With a text that read "Adios mi vida"

"Adios, mi vida," she texted back with her henna-painted fingers. With teary eyes, she saw Gautam in front of her. This will be her life, and it's time that she accepts it.

The day ended with the Haldi ceremony. Everyone was so tired that they slept unconsciously.

It was the Devil's hour when the phone buzzed ferociously: grrrr...grrrr...grrrr.

Only a few minutes ago she dived into deep sleep. Her mind had already entered into the subconscious stage, but one part of the brain was still receptive to what was happening in the surroundings.

'Open the eyes,' the mind was signalling her, but she was in another episode of sleep paralysis.

After struggling for a few minutes, she opened her eyes and reached out to get her phone; it was tucked under her sister's bum.

"Sleep, Aaru, there's a lot to do tomorrow." Saying that, her sister turned towards the other side, and she grabbed her phone.

It was a number that was not saved in her contacts, but she could remember it even in her next life, if there is one.

With some trepidation, she unlocked her phone; there was a voicemail that said, *"We met with an accident."*

It was a bolt from the blue for her. She struggled to breathe heavily, so shocked that she couldn't move an inch. She could feel her brain fading, as if she was turning into a rock.

What she heard in the voice note devastated her.

They say be careful of what you wish for; was it because she wished for something like this? Can she have it all? Or had she just lost everything?

She collected herself somehow and searched for her car keys. After searching and throwing all the stuff out of her bag, it clicked that she always keeps a spare key in her bag's secret pocket. She rushed out of the room and ran towards her car when Sujith, who was still awake, saw her. "Arannya! Wait." He ran to her and asked what happened.

"Ray! He met with an accident." She said in a trembling voice, "Let me drive," he said, and they went to the hospital Ray mentioned in another voicemail. Since Sujith's phone was not reachable, he asked her to tell him to be there.

Arannya was panic-stricken; she was calling back on his number, but he wasn't answering.

"Aaru, don't worry; we'll get there soon. Till then, keep trying his phone," said Sujith.

Both Sujith and Arannya couldn't think straight at the moment and wanted to reach the hospital as soon as possible. All the memories of her birthday when Kartik met with an accident came flooding in her mind and she started sobbing.

When they reached, Arannya opened the car's door simultaneously while Sujith hit the brakes and ran inside the hospital. "Ray, I'm looking for Ray, car accident." She enquired in a shaky voice.

"Narayan, where is he?" Sujith asked the reception.

"They are in the emergency ward." Arannya rushed to find the emergency ward while Sujith did the formalities. His wife was undergoing an emergency surgery. She saw Ray half conscious, surrounded by doctors and nurses.

"Ray!" she said in a low voice. She walked to him, and a few doctors walked out of the room mentioning some surgery.

"Who was on duty?" The doctor asked.

"Why hasn't he been given a phenytoin yet?!" The doctor reprimanded the trainees.

Ray was slowly losing his consciousness, but as he saw Arannya, he was trying to speak something. Wanted to ask her why she is here when he has asked Sujith to come.

He saw that she was coloured yellow. Her henna was not yet washed off her hands completely.

She went near him and wanted to talk, but words found it difficult to find a way out of her mouth; they were choked in the throat because of the trauma. Tears also seemed to forget their way out of her eyes.

The trench coat that he was wearing was stained with his blood and was kept on the sofa beside him. He pointed his fingers to it. Arannya picked it up and started to search its pockets. In the pocket inside there was something; when she pulled it, she couldn't hold herself any longer and broke down.

It was the same scarf that she lost at the party when Ray first spoke to her.

She held his hands and was crying helplessly.

"What's happening here?" The nurse came inside and told Arannya not to disturb the patient and asked her to wait outside.

"Go, it's your wedding today." He said in a cracky voice. She shook her head in rejection.

"I won't until you get better!" she stated.

"I promise, I will, if you go now. Otherwise it's better that I...." He was cut short as Arannya closed his mouth with her hands before he said anything further.

"Madam! Don't you understand? Get out, please!" The nurse ordered. Sujith was watching this from behind.

She took the scarf tied to his wrist, kissed his hand, and came outside crying.

Sujith came near Ray.

"How is she?" Ray asked.

"Everything will be fine. Bhai, I am here; don't worry." Sujith consoled him.

"Arannya..." Ray was concerned.

"I will send her back. You please don't stress out."

Sujith has already informed Gautam. He was on his way to the hospital to take Arannya back.

She had refused Sujith before he came, but he made her understand that if she doesn't go, Ray will be stressed, and at this point she has to listen to him.

Her well-being was his strength. And his wish, her command.

Gautam came and took Arannya with him.

He did not complain about anything. Since he didn't want to create a scene, he told everyone in the family that Arannya was with him. Gautam was like a perfect man, how to handle a situation nobody knew better than him. Arannya lost all her senses. Gautam told Lax about the situation and asked her to be with Arannya at all times.

Gautam asked Lax to take her inside her room and told his family she wanted to have a morning walk, so he took her to the plateau. He reasoned it with cold feet, which were common during such times.

Their parents sniffed something was wrong but, given the current situation, did not pursue further interrogation.

Throughout the day, Arannya was on the phone with Sujith. The makeup artist came; Lax asked to keep it minimal.

"Madam, it will look too plain for a bride," said the MUA.

"Do as suggested, please," Lax said.

Shiney arrived just in time with Vishal. Shiney had a surprise for her; she was getting engaged to Vishal. But when Lax told Shiney about what happened, her excitement was gone for a toss, and she asked everyone to be left alone with Arannya.

"Shiney!" She saw her and burst into tears.

"Shh, what did I tell you? No emotional attachment. You are ruining the most important day of your life, Arannya!" Shiny schooled her.

"I may sound inhuman. But he is under the doctor's supervision and will be fine today or tomorrow. But the bruise you will give Gautam because of your behaviour will never heal, I tell you. Stop being so selfish and think about him for once. Forget about that. Will you be able to live with the guilt of hurting him and make eye contact with him after this?" Shiney tried to knock some sense into her.

"I know my friend won't let her parents down." Shiney said and hugged her. "Let me meet Uncle and Aunty and apologise to them for showing up at the last minute."

She went out to meet Arannya's parents and see if she could be of any help.

It was 8 PM. Arannya was calling Sujith, but his phone was switched off. She called the hospital to check; the reception personnel told her they don't have any information regarding the patient and requested she call the relative who is there in the hospital.

She called Ray's number; his phone must be with Sujith, she thought. But it was unanswered.

Arannya began to feel knots in her stomach. She sensed something untoward had happened. The makeup artist was doing some final touch-ups. Arannya's legs were shaking continuously in anxiety. "Didi Could you please go and call Lax? She's not answering my calls", she requested the MUA. The makeup artist didn't like it, but she obliged her customer and went out to search for Lax.

Arannya got a call from Ray. She answered within a second.

"Hello," she said.

There was silence from the other side. But in that span of time, hundreds of thoughts made their way into her mind.

"Ray?" She called his name.

Still no answer.

"We... lost... him... We lost him..." Sujith's trembling words caved in her world.

What she heard was like getting shot at point-blank. The phone slipped from her hand.

She took the blade, which she had earlier noticed in the MUA's emergency kit, and locked herself inside the washroom.

Whatever she was doing was for him. Even though they could never be together, they both know the love they have for each other was enough reason to sustain this life. There were no promises made between them, just the shared feelings and emotions flowing in the similar rhythm.

The fact that the love of their life is still under the same sun, even though hundreds of miles away, gave them a hope that maybe someday, when the universe would feel pity on them, it would orchestrate the events to unite them forever. Until then, they would continue living their life, hanging on, hoping for a miracle.

But now, now what? What does she have to lose? She closed her eyes and visualised her time with Ray in his house, her fondest memory of all. She held the blade steady and, without any second thoughts, ran it across her left hand's veins and collapsed.

The colour of their love was verily white, but what kind of love does not have a little bit of red involved?

People may call it madness, but isn't madness the closest synonym to love?

Thick, dark, and red, the floor is covered in blood; one could hear banging on the door and people screaming outside the bathroom. After a few attempts, the door was broken open, and they were aghast to see Arannya lying unconscious on the floor, blood oozing out of her hand profusely.

She was rushed to the hospital.

Gautam was dumbfounded; eventually he was cognisant that loving her on her terms couldn't be enough reason for her to stay.

No amount of love can be at par with the love the heart actually yearns for. No amount of love can match even a tiny amount of what the heart desires. Oftentimes, people accept the defeat and relish what they've been served, but no other form of drink can really quench the thirst like water does, can it?

Love in itself is no lesser than a disease, and no matter how illogical or immoral it may be, its cure lies in the embrace of what it truly desires.

For the heart doesn't have any cognitive ability. It operates on vibrations felt by the known souls around.

Ergo, the heart wants what it wants.

Finding the four leaf clover

One aspect of life that is usually underestimated is the people around us, irrespective of whether or not we know them. We tend to think that the lives or deeds of those strangers to us have no significant impact on our lives. But come to think of it, it has a larger impact. Imagine what would happen if the person evaluating your answer sheet had just had a spat with their partner and took it out on your scores. Imagine the doctor you went to for a diagnosis wrongly prescribes you based on the blood report, which was an outcome of manhandled samples of blood by the staff in the pathology lab, just because he/she wanted to take out the frustration of all the times they were mistreated by this world. Imagine what would happen if the pilot of the plane you boarded is suicidal.

Scary enough!? But if we keep on suspecting each and everyone around us, how will we ever be able to live? Trust comes into play here and encourages us to just go on with life. Thus, people around us have a deeper impact on our lives than we can fathom.

Isn't it astonishing to know how suddenly one mistake of a drunken truck driver changed the course of life entirely for three individuals?

"*Then darling, you become that person,*" answered a fragile and very low reminiscing voice to Rishu when she asked the same question to Arannya, which she had asked her Dadu when he told her the moral of the Idgah story.

Forty years later, in her twilight years, Arannya understood the true meaning of what her Dadu meant when he said those lines. Throughout her life, she thought of becoming the one to love someone more than herself when she failed to find someone who loved her more than themselves. But what her Dadu meant was she has to become that person for herself.

"Tell me, Nanny, what if I don't find such a person?" asked Rishu.

"Then darling, you become that person.... for yourself," she added.

"Capisce?" Arannya asked.

"Ah-haan." Rishu nodded.

"Run along now and ask Minu didi for a glass of milk." She caressed her and got up from her bed with some effort.

Old age never fails to work upon even the finest of genes. She was no exception; it was just that she was ageing at a much slower rate.

Arannya, who is now seventy, was taking a walk down memory lane, looking at the pictures on a wall dedicated to the photographs of all her major events in life. She saw the picture of her marriage with Gautam; there was a bandage on her hand and she looked lost, and her eyes were glued to the carpet while Gautam was adjusting her hair. That day still remains as one of the hardest in her life. Then she saw a picture of their baby boy, Gaurang, of course a name resembling both of their names by conjugating. This has almost become a ritual in her family, and most of the couples then, even if the name makes absolutely no sense, kept their baby's name by joining theirs.

And Gautam wasn't asexual but a graysexual. However, after copulating for the first time and making her conceive, he turned completely asexual. Then she saw a picture where she gifted a sports car to Gautam on his 40th birthday with a sash over him that read Naughty at forty. He looked extremely elated. Then she saw a picture of Yana in her hands, where she was crying and Yana was cooing happily.

"Where's the French press? I am making coffee; would you like some?" He announced from the kitchen. She got distracted.

"Someone woke up from the wrong side of the bed today! And if you've decided to hit the kitchen, then please make tea, honey." she said as she requested and went to the patio gazebo, which was placed in the front yard.

There were several chairs of different shapes and sizes and a special long and relaxing armchair made from the nicest African blackwood for him.

She looked at the beautiful garden around her and how the sun rays falling on them made it shine like the garden of Hesperides.

He came holding the tray with teacups, taking careful steps.

"Why didn't you ask Minu to get these here?" She looked annoyed.

"It's okay, don't underestimate my capabilities! I can still make women go weak in their knees." He faked an arrogant tone and placed the tray on the table. And took something from his pocket.

"Look what I found," he said and gave it to her.

"You still have it!" She was surprised.

"Just not in its original state; blame the cloth moths."

Ray said and passed the silk geometric print scarf, which he picked at the party where they first interacted.

A teardrop fell from her eye and landed on the scarf.

She kissed the scarf and placed it neatly on the table, securing it under the newspaper.

"Drink and tell me how it is," asked Ray.

"Perfecto," she said and passed him a flying kiss.

"How are Gautam and Kritika?" he asked.

"I spoke to him yesterday; he was asking from which doctor I got my cataract surgery done," she said and continued, "Kritika seems to be in pain because her slip disc is giving her hell!"

"When did you say Gaurang is coming here?" He asked.

"Nothing is confirmed; he is impulsive like me; his plans are ever-changing. But I am hoping for next week." She answered.

"And Yana?" He asked.

"What about her?" She questioned back.

"Haven't you spoken to her?" he asked.

"I did," she said casually.

"Then tell me how she is!" He seemed irked.

"Isn't she your daughter too? Why don't you guys end this feud and reconcile?" she charged.

"Aarna, she is being irrational by accepting the offer of being an on-field war reporter. How do you want me to give consent to this?" he asked.

"Don't drag me into this. She is our daughter after all; do you expect her to take traditional ways to life? I gave up on this thought the day she opened her eyes in the world, refused to cry, and smiled instead!" She said as she slurped her tea.

A young boy in his early thirties taking his morning walk stopped by and greeted them, "Good morning, Dadaji; good morning, Aunty."

"Good morning, Beta," they said concurrently.

"Why are you an aunty and I dadaji?" Ray was fairly jealous.

"Good genes, hon!" She mocked him.

"By the way, Krishaan and his wife will be coming in a couple of weeks to take Rishu back and also take the papers of your hometown's property," she informed Ray.

"Why are they taking her back so soon?" Ray got irritated.

"She has school to attend too! You know how excited she is for fifth grade as she'll get to use fountain pens." She smiled softly.

"Hmmm." He replied, engrossed in deep thoughts. She read his mind and said.

"Ray, I know how difficult it is for you to sell that property, but everything yours is ultimately Krishaan's, right?" she said.

"And what about Yana? Isn't she my daughter? Our Daughter? She's always been discriminated against by our families. I will give whatever Krishaan wants, but this house, which we have built together, will be hers to keep, and that's final," he stated.

"Okay, I am sorry. Calm down now; I will get your meds," she said and went inside.

While coming back, the medicine bottle slipped from her hand and landed on the lawn. When she went to pick it up, she saw a trail of wildly grown clovers in between the wedelias. As she bent to pick up the bottle, there, she saw the four-leaf clover for the first time in her life.

Her happiness knew no bounds. She plucked it and was engrossed in observing it minutely. She was looking at the leaf, which looked ordinary to her eyes but was extraordinary for her heart. How she used to frantically search for this in her early years, how this little thing defied the Fibonacci sequence and sprouted right in her own garden, really mesmerised her.

"Look what I found!!!!" she exclaimed.

"Finally! Ray, please come here. Look!!! The four-leaf clover! I found it! I found it!" She exclaimed and was on cloud nine.

When Ray did not answer. She called him again; after the third time, she got up as the tendons in her knees made a weird sound and took the cloverleaf for him to see.

As she reached the gazebo, her excitement vanished when she saw a broken teacup on the floor and an unconscious Ray holding the scarf. She could see there was peace on his face.

She kneeled and took the scarf from his hands and tied it to his wrist.

She put the four-leaf clover in his palm and closed it.

She found the four-leaf clover at that exact moment she lost the love of her life, only this time, forever.

"Adios, mi vida," she kissed as she bid her ultimate adieu.

Ray was terminally ill. He was under palliative care. Yana, '*ArannYANArayan*', a child with a contradicting personality, like their name Yes and No, two antitheses, was their daughter, born out of wedlock; they never got married. They never felt the necessity to make their love governed by the law. How they ended up being together is another epic saga of revenge, lust, betrayal, loss, and love. Maybe someday, when the world is ready to fathom the kind of love Arannya and Narayan had towards each other, will be the day it shall be told. The story of '*Finding the missing leaf*'.

Until then, let's keep on the lookout for our four-leaf clover. Define what each petal means for us, and find the missing one to have a fulfilling life.

In Arannya's life, it was Love. But she had the courage to change her fate and fight against all odds to get what was hers and find the missing leaf to her clover, her love. She indeed fell in the fifth category. With a life lived full of Hope, Faith, Luck, and Love, she found her four-leaf clover.

Being at the brink of shattering forever, she chose to lock horns with the world, she fought; she fought until she won, and then she had it all.

All her life she thought that she was ordinary and love is something that isn't meant for her; but with an extraordinary heart, she made it possible.

Love indeed is not for the ordinary but for some extraordinary fools like them.

Arannya-Narayan, two inseparable souls whose destiny was penned before they came into this life. Two lovers so unique that even their names had the same letters in exact numbers. How can they ever not be united? For when something is meant to be, it's meant to be. Don't you agree?

Arannya and Narayan loved each other more than themselves. And you'd know my answer if you'd ask me, What if you don't find the one who loves you more than themselves?

"Then darling, you become that person."

"Capisce?"

"The years of life spent without being in love are an absolute waste." - Bhavana Poly

Know Your Author

"I am a writer; I need my hand," was the first thing a 22-year-old girl said after being rescued from a fatal accident, which broke the humerus bone of her dominant hand. A dream that was conceived during childhood never really abandoned her subconscious. Life went on, and the will to break away from being financially dependent got the best of her. After years of helping her friends and family with emails, cover letters, speeches, and even personal replies, she decided to let her creative juices flow and follow her passion.

This is Bhavana Kapse's alias, Bhavana Poly's, first foray into storytelling. Born in Chandrapur, Maharashtra, an asset manager in a media firm, she is listed on IMDb for her stint in VFX and currently resides in Bangalore.

She can be contacted at:
IG: bhavanapoly
E-mail: bhavana.poly@gmail.com
Website: bhavanapoly.in

www.ingramcontent.com/pod-product-compliance
Lightning Source LLC
LaVergne TN
LVHW091627070526
838199LV00044B/969